Tagged

Her new boss isn't the only threat on the streets...

Unfinished Business
Book 2

Juanita Kees

Tagged
Juanita Kees

Her new boss isn't the only threat on the streets...

TJ Stevens will go to any lengths to protect the young offenders in her apprenticeship rehabilitation program. She's worked hard to keep them off the streets and out of trouble. With her new boss threatening to cancel the program and danger striking close to home for the youths, will Scott Devin be a trusted ally or yet another enemy?

When Scott Devin buys a struggling car dealership in semi-rural Western Australia, he knows he's buying a bucketload of trouble. He's just not expecting the mess he walks in on, or the reason for it. Heading up the challenge is a woman who fights like a tigress protecting her cubs against the dark underworld of crime. Can he afford to get involved in the danger she brings to his door?

About The Author

Finding hope in country towns with dark secrets ...

Juanita escapes the real world to create emotionally engaging stories steeped in crime, suspense, mystery and intrigue. Her books are set in dusty, rural outback Australia and on the NASCAR racetracks of America. Her small-town USA and Australian rural stories have made the Amazon bestseller and top 100 lists. Juanita also likes to dabble in the ponds of fantasy and paranormal with Greek gods brought to life in the 21st century.

Juanita graduated college with distinctions and a diploma in Proofreading, Editing and Publishing in 2011 and started her freelance writing business, Kees2Create Words. As a developmental and structural editor, she assists writers to polish their manuscripts for submission. In 2012, she achieved her dream of becoming a published author and now has multiple novels on the market.

When she's not working, writing, editing or proofreading, Juanita enjoys travelling to discover new worlds for inspiration. Mother to two handsome heroes and partner to a car enthusiast, Juanita also has a passion for fast cars and country living.

Juanita loves to talk books with readers and would love to connect. Contact her via:

Amazon Author:
https://www.amazon.com/author/juanitakees
Website:
https://juanitakees.com/contact/
Kees2Create Words Editing:
https://kees2createwords.com/
Bookbub:
https://www.bookbub.com/authors/juanita-kees
Newsletter:
https://kees2createwords.substack.com/embed
Goodreads:
https://www.goodreads.com/author/show/6454477.
Juanita_Kees
Book Love Book Club: https://www.facebook.com/
groups/607880523038543

Acknowledgments

Australian businessman and politician JJ Simons founded the Young Australia League and established a holiday camp deep in the shaded Roleystone valley in 1929. Simons called his camp Araluen, an Eastern States Aboriginal word meaning 'singing waters,' 'running waters' or 'place of lilies'. Together, League members and volunteers built cottages, designed by leading Perth architect WG Bennett, using local timber and stone. They created pathways, roads, steps and terraces and filled the dream garden with native and imported plants to create a garden heaven.

The Grove of the Unforgotten still remains today, built in memory of Young Australia League members killed in World War I.

Now known as Araluen Botanical Park, this has to be the most peaceful garden in Western Australia. Many of the cottages have been restored, except for one that burnt down, leaving only the chimney stack standing.

http://www.araluenbotanicpark.com.au/about/

I chose a similar setting for TJ & Scott's story, because of its history and original purpose. How wonderful would it be if young people could return to this peaceful place while they search for themselves through the trials of growing up?

Unfortunately, my story is fiction and TJ is no relation to JJ Simons, but his dream and my love for his creation provided the perfect background for this story of an extraordinary woman who has her own dream and a commitment that knows no boundaries. I hope you enjoy the story.

For my Uncle Alan

I'll always be your little tiger. You'll never know how much your solid presence meant as I struggled through my teenage years

and Aunty Rochelle

for helping Uncle Alan find his 'happy ever after'

Contents

Chapter One

TJ pushed through the doors into the reception area of Mal's Motors, leaving them swinging behind her. 'Marty, I need a tow down on Albany Highway. Sheila's spat the dummy again,' she yelled. Her car was getting too old and unreliable to be out late. She'd pushed Sheila too hard last night, scouring the streets, looking for Tiny. She had no other choice, but a car that could break down at any time placed her in a vulnerable position in the dark alleyways where her boys found most of their trouble. Or rather, where trouble found them.

A man in a suit stepped in front of her. 'Are you TJ Stevens?'

'Yes. Sorry, I'll be with you in just a moment.'

TJ missed the disgruntled look he aimed her way as she set her hands on his forearms and steered him out of her path. She grabbed her uniform jacket off the peg and heaved open the connecting door to the workshop. There'd been no sign of Tiny, despite searching until almost dawn, and now she was over-tired from lack of sleep and later than late. 'Marty!'

'I got it, TJ,' the first-year apprentice yelled back.

'Take Tony with you. You know she won't let anyone else near her.'

'Got it.' Marty jogged toward her with a tow rope looped over his shoulder. 'There's someone to see you out front. Not happy that you're late.' He nodded toward the man she'd moved aside, who now paced the reception floor.

TJ tossed Marty her keys. 'I'll take care of it. Go and get Sheila before she gets a ticket. Tony! Let's get this done. We've got a big workload today.' She gave them directions to the broken-down car. 'Marty, have you seen Tiny lately?'

'Nah, TJ. I'm doing like you said and staying out of trouble.'

'Good lad. You'll let me know if he tries to contact you though, right?'

'Yeah, you know I will.'

'Cool. Go get my car now so we can start the day.'

With a sigh, she headed for the cloakroom and sat down on the bench to unstrap her stiletto sandals. The day hadn't even started yet, and already she had blisters. Not helped at all by the two-kilometre hike, thanks to Sheila breaking down. She tugged on her uniform pants under her mini skirt.

Her mobile phone vibrated against the cold steel bench, the display showing an unknown caller. It skittered off the edge to fall face down in the greasy mop bucket. Luckily, the water had been drained.

'Looks like it's going to be one of those days.' Resigned to her fate, she fished her phone out of the grey sludge and wiped it on a rag.

'TJ? The bloke in reception says you need to get your butt out there now.' One of the technicians banged on the cloakroom door.

'I'll be out in a minute.' Work-worn, scarred safety boots replaced the heels, hastily tugged on over thick socks. The laces could wait. TJ strode back into the workshop, laces flapping against the concrete floor as she went.

'Back to work,' she called when she noticed that work had ground to a halt as her team watched her progress across the shop. TJ smiled at the comments, cat calls, grumbles and exaggerated sighs.

'Sheila ready for the scrap heap this time?'

'Blown a gasket has she?'

'Forget something, TJ?'

As leading hand, she was used to the teasing. The

relationship she had with her team was a good one. They worked well together.

The connecting door back into the reception didn't budge as she shoved against it with her bottom and simultaneously tried to secure her wayward hair in a rubber band.

'Ouch,' she muttered just as it gave way, and two firm hands grasped her shoulders. The hands spun her around firmly. She looked up. A long way up. The muscular frame of her impatient visitor blocked the doorway.

'Tiffany-Jane Stevens?' His voice reverberated through her, deep and rumbling. Not unlike thunder — which matched the expression on his face.

She shivered. 'Yes?'

'Scott Devin. Tie your damn shoes, take off that ridiculous skirt, and meet me in my office.' He spun around and stalked off.

Shit! TJ stared at his departing back with a sinking feeling in her stomach. Scott Devin. Her new boss. He was a week early. It was definitely going to be a bad day.

Scott slammed the door to his predecessor's office. As if he didn't have enough on his plate already, he'd arrived at his newly acquired dealership at 7.30am to find the place locked up, no staff, and customers queuing at the door. If it wasn't for the set of keys the agent had given him at handover, they'd all still be out on the driveway awaiting the arrival of his leading hand.

He hated to be kept waiting, especially when he had so much to do. Irritation ripped through him. She hadn't even recognised him as her new boss because she'd been so focused on using his staff to tow her own car. And to set him aside like that ... What if he'd been a customer? No wonder Mal's Motors was in trouble. Which was just one of the reasons he was here. Voted Most Successful Businessman of the Year, he'd acquired several struggling car dealerships nationwide and turned them into multi-million-dollar enterprises.

He picked up the latest edition of *Professional Spotlight* then tossed it aside again with a grunt. His face stared back at him from the cover, silent and brooding. Here he was in the foothills of Perth with his latest acquisition, but, instead of feeling the usual drive to turn it around, he felt unsettled.

Somewhere in the rat race on the east coast, he'd lost his passion for doing what he did. And the reason for that still posed a threat, even as far away as across the country. He stared out the window at the hills in the distance. If only he could make the last twelve months go away.

He'd thought he'd find a new challenge in a dealership that had once been a country workshop. Now it was surrounded by a growing suburb on the main highway into Perth. Favoured by the locals, it maintained its country atmosphere, with all the facilities of a small town. The potential for growth was huge and the challenge was certainly there. Would it be enough to start over?

A firm tap on his door heralded the arrival of Tiffany-Jane Stevens. He shook his head and squared his shoulders. He'd not expected TJ Stevens to be a pint-sized, stiletto-wearing cannon ball in a mini skirt who arrived late to work, left customers out in the cold and her employees unsupervised.

'Come in.'

TJ opened the door and strode up to his desk, hands firmly on her hips. 'Mr Devin, I'm sorry I was late and not here to greet you, but I have a huge workload today, so can we hurry this up? I'm happy to set a meeting with you after closing time.'

She'd tied her boots and taken off the skirt. Her hi-vis work jacket remained unzipped, *Here Comes Trouble* printed in black on the grey T-shirt she wore underneath it. Scott pulled out his chair and sat down. Her T-shirt said it all.

'No kidding,' he muttered.

'I beg your pardon?' TJ looked at him uncertainly.

'Sit down, TJ.'

'I'd rather stand if that's okay with you?' Green eyes clashed with his. 'I'm running a bit behind.'

He stood up again. 'Punctuality is important in a leading hand. You're meant to be setting an example for your team.'

She narrowed her gaze on his face. 'My car broke down. It's not like I overslept.'

Scott acknowledged the tinge of sarcasm behind her words, but he pushed on. 'Your car broke down. Did you think to ring someone and let them know?'

TJ shook her head. 'My phone battery is running low. I need to put it on charge.'

'Perhaps you should have thought of that before you left a nightclub to come straight to work. You were an hour late!' How else could she explain the mini skirt and stilettos at 8.30 in the morning?

'Is that where you think I've come from?' Her back stiffened, drawing her to her full height of just over five foot. She sucked in her bottom lip and chewed on it, clearly biting back an angry response. 'You know what? You're right, of course. I'm sorry. It won't happen again.'

'Damn straight, it won't happen again. You also broke a few safety rules.' He ticked them off on his fingers. 'You didn't secure your shoe laces before entering the workspace, presenting a trip hazard. You wore a frilly skirt over your protective wear, presenting a snarl hazard, and you traipsed across a greasy floor in open-toed, *stiletto heels*!' His irritation escalated as he counted off her sins.

Scott watched her face pale as the implications dawned. She was the team leader, the one to set the example. Breaking safety rules could mean only one thing. 'You're fired.' He delivered the final blow and sat back down. 'Pack up your things. I'll have HR make up your severance package.' He tried not to feel like an arsehole as she quietly turned and left the office.

'Egotistical, pompous, east coast *arse*!' Seething, TJ marched back into the workshop. She hated it when people made assumptions. 'Meeting, boys.' She waved the team over to the clocking machine. They downed their tools and gathered around her. 'That was your new boss. I've been fired.' She held up a hand to stem the grumbled responses. 'No, he's right. I broke the rules. When Tony gets back, he'll take over as team leader until Mr Devin finds a replacement for me. I expect you all to respect his wishes and work with him.'

'But, TJ, what about our contracts?' Terry tipped back his cap to rub at his shaved head. 'We don't want to work with anyone else.'

TJ's heart hitched. She'd worked so hard to get Terry off meth. Two years later, he was on the straight and narrow, enrolled in a mature-aged apprenticeship, and mentoring the younger kids.

'I'll still be around. Just not here. No setbacks, guys.

We've worked too hard to let the program slide. It's all up to you now.' She stopped as she saw their eyes shift to the observation window where customers could watch the work being carried out from the safety of the reception area.

Scott Devin stood watching. Probably making sure she left the premises without stealing anything. The sour thought ran through her mind even as her skin tingled from the force of his gaze boring into her back. She stiffened her spine. TJ snapped her fingers in the air and drew her team's attention back to her. 'Guys! Tony will need your support.'

They nodded their agreement, just as Tony strode into the shop. 'What's going on?'

'You're in charge.'

Terry pushed his cap back on. 'That new arsehole just fired her.'

'What? Why?' Tony looked up to where Scott stood behind the glass.

He made to push past TJ toward the reception, but she held him back. 'Let it go, mate.'

'But TJ, he has no idea —'

'Let it go. He'll find out soon enough. I'll have to leave Sheila here overnight. I'll arrange for a tow truck in the morning. Back to work now, guys.' She waved them away.

Tony stood his ground. 'It's not fair.'

'It's the rules. How bad is Sheila?'

Tony shook his head. 'Hard to say. She smelled a little burnt. We'll have to take the cylinder head off for pressure testing. Lucky you know not to push her too far when she starts overheating. Hopefully the damage will be minimal.' He indicated with a thumb over his shoulder to the driveway. 'Marty's just getting her settled.'

She hooked an arm through Tony's and steered him out the workshop onto the drive. Out the corner of her eye, she saw Scott Devin on the move too. As heart-stoppingly gorgeous in person as he was in the magazine, he towered at least a foot or more over her, built like a brick wall. The tailored business suit enhanced rather than hid the strong, muscular body underneath. Chiselled features tapered into a round jaw darkened by stubble, a slightly crooked nose and dark blue eyes that could stop a freight train in its tracks with just one look. Jet black hair cut neat and short … It didn't matter how attractive he was, he was still a pompous arse.

They stepped out onto the driveway where Sheila sat, offering an occasional hiss and spit. Steam still floated through the radiator grille. The 1975 Holden Gemini SL Sedan was a patchwork of faded red and body filler grey. Clear lacquer blistered in the areas that had not been filled. Once restoration was complete, she would be a collector's item for enthusiasts. For TJ, even worthless, it was one of her most valued possessions.

'*This* is your car?' Scott stepped up next to her.

She looked up at him, desperately wanting to wipe the smirk off his face. Instead, she moved to lift the bonnet. 'Marty, hit the release cable.' She pulled her heat resistant gloves out of her pocket and put them on.

'Now she remembers the safety rules,' Scott muttered.

TJ stiffened until she thought her spine would snap but ignored him. She had nothing more to lose. Only good manners made her bite down on a response. There was no reason to give him the satisfaction. She lifted the bonnet and secured it with the metal stay. Bracing her hands on the front of the car, she leaned in to look for broken fan belts or a damaged fan blade. None. That was good.

'No blown hoses, TJ.' Tony snapped off his torch. 'Radiator's leaking through the core. Probably warped the cylinder head a little.'

'Let's hope it's only a little.' TJ stepped back and straightened. She felt Scott's muscular warmth at her back where he'd been peering over her shoulder.

'As riveting as this is, can we all get back to work now? We're running a little behind schedule.'

She swallowed the sarcasm she wanted to respond with. TJ turned to face him. 'Yes. I'll get her picked up in the morning if it's okay for her to stay overnight?'

He shrugged. 'Do I have a choice?'

'Yes, you can say no.' She pulled off her gloves and

shoved them into his chest, leaving him no option but to close his hands around them. Her patience was running out fast. TJ pushed past him. 'Marty, have you still got my keys?'

'Yep, why?'

'Toolbox key is the third one in. Go inside and pack up my tools, please.'

'Say what, TJ?' Marty stopped dead in the middle of dropping Sheila's bonnet back into place.

'I don't work here anymore. Tony, can you please drop off my toolbox on your way home tonight?' TJ patted Marty on the back. 'Tony will take care of you, Marty.'

'Sure, TJ, but —' The terror on the boy's face made her heart ache. She was the one who picked him up every time he got sucked back into back-alley business.

She dropped her hand onto his shoulder. 'It's okay, Marty. You've got my number. Call me whenever you need to.'

Marty dropped the bonnet a little harder than necessary and stormed off into the shop, his shoulders rigid as he swore under his breath.

'That'll be 20c in the swear jar, mate. Tony, you've got this, right?'

Tony shot Scott Devin a look of pure contempt before answering. 'Sure, TJ. Drop off the toolbox, take care of Marty and Sheila.'

'Back to work then. You've got a shop to run.'

He aimed another killer look at the new boss before he complied.

TJ pulled her mobile phone out of her pocket and dialled.

Silence hung heavily as she waited for an answer. She couldn't resist a look at Scott. He held her gaze until she looked away.

'Rob, I need a lift home. Yes, now. I'll explain when you get here.' She pressed the screen to end the call. 'I'll just get dressed and then I'll get out of your hair.'

'You do that, Tiger,' he answered as she walked away.

Chapter Two

'Why is that damn car still here?' Scott asked Tony later the next day. Sheila stood outside on the drive where she'd come to a halt the day before. 'I thought she was being towed.' The cost to tow the car would be more than it was worth. He realised he was starting to feel sympathetic. It was all TJ's fault. He'd spent a restless night wondering if he'd made a mistake by firing her. The image of her and her car had kept him awake long after his forgotten beer was warm. That wasn't a good sign.

Tony eyed Scott coldly. 'Trouble with the tow truck. Still need to drop off TJ's toolbox.' Despite the team's best efforts, the workshop had not run smoothly without TJ. They'd worked long past knock-off time to get the workload out. 'Late night last night.'

'Yes, I know. You handled it well.' After a long, awkward pause Scott asked, 'Something else you want to say, Tony?'

'We'd have handled it better with TJ in charge.'

'And?'

Tony hesitated. 'How far do I push it before you fire me too? You've shown yourself to be a hard nut, Mr Devin, but without TJ at the helm, things could go very wrong. So, I'm going to go for broke here and hope I'll still have a job next week to feed my kids. I think you made a mistake firing her. TJ would never do anything to put anyone in danger. She's the first one in and last one to go when Sheila's not playing up.'

'Does she play up often?'

Tony hesitated again, scratching his head. 'Not sure if you mean TJ or Sheila. Either way, it's been a worse week than usual.'

'Right, and the rest of the team? Do they share your opinion of TJ?'

Tony shrugged. 'Some of the boys have started talking about quitting. A couple have already written out their resignations. Most of them are only here for one reason, and that's TJ. There's a lot about her and what she does here that you don't know. I'd bet my morning tea that Mal didn't pass on much information at takeover.'

'Care to enlighten me?'

'It's not my place to say anything that will betray

TJ's confidences. But I will ask this … are you serious about turning this place around?'

'I'm a businessman, Tony. I wouldn't have invested in it if I wasn't.'

'Then you need to understand that this isn't just another business. It may not be turning over a huge profit, but sometimes there's more to it than money. TJ has worked hard to keep this place together. She's not the one responsible for the lack of profit. But she is the reason most of us are here.' Tony dug a key out of his pocket and dangled it by the metal ring. 'If you want to know more, ask the right questions and get answers from the right people. Offer her the job back or take her toolbox back to her yourself.'

Scott held out his hand to catch the key as it dropped. He looked at it where it lay in his palm before closing his fist around the cool metal. 'I might just do that.'

Tony turned and walked toward the workshop. He stopped when Scott said, 'Tony, I appreciate your honesty. Tell the team to hold fire. I'll talk to TJ.'

Even at the height of the nastiest takeover bid, he'd never been a mean bastard. Had he got it so wrong?

The cold weight of the key in his palm reminded him of TJ's banged up car. Scott walked out to where Sheila stood silent, lifeless in the sun. He opened the driver's door and slid inside.

The contents of the glove box had spilled all over

the passenger side floor. TJ had rifled through it before leaving the day before. The lock on the glove box must have broken when she'd slammed it shut. It was the only indication of a temper she'd kept tightly controlled. He admired that.

He leaned over to scoop up the bits and pieces, making a mental note to place them in a bag and return them to TJ. As he dropped them on the seat, a photograph caught his eye. In it, TJ stood with two men between an old FJ Holden Utility and Sheila. Sunlight shone on her hair, highlighting the strands of gold among the titian. Her heart-shaped face glowed with happiness in the photograph, unlike the thunderous scowl he'd been faced with in his office yesterday.

Scott dropped the photograph onto the seat. Had he been too hasty in his judgement of her? When had he become such a hard arse? He could blame it on the trouble he'd left behind on the east coast, but that would be unfair. He'd never allowed his personal life to mix with business. Not until he'd met Serena, and that's when it had all gone to hell. Lesson learned.

He got out and slammed the door. A rivet from the door handle fell and spun desolately around his feet. A metallic groan rent the air. He had no time to realise its source before Sheila neatly dropped her front bumper on his foot. The car was old and falling apart. Scott kicked the bumper aside. 'Yeah, not at all sure you're really worth fixing, Sheila.'

Scott set the alarm as he locked the dealership door for the night. He'd been putting it off the whole day, but eventually he'd run out of excuses. He'd decided not to take TJ's toolbox to her. Instead, he would see what she had to say first — if she would talk to him. There was no harm in giving her the opportunity to apologise. She'd been the one breaking the rules after all. Although, in all fairness, he had been a little hasty in firing her. He could have given her a written warning instead.

As he strode out to his ute, he fumbled in his pocket for the crumpled piece of paper Tony had scribbled TJ's address onto. 'Rowley's Gum Nut Cottage, Karingal Crescent, Karalee.' He swore loudly. 'Damned if she's not Mum's neighbour. Seriously?' If he believed in the gods, he'd swear they were laughing down on him right now.

He hadn't visited Mum and Dad's haven in the hills yet. They'd opted for the tree change while he'd been tied up with settling the messy business over east. He shrugged out of his jacket and removed his tie, tossing them both carelessly into the passenger seat before loosening the top two buttons of his shirt. He rolled up the sleeves and sat with his hands on the steering wheel for a few minutes as he wondered what he would say to TJ when he got there. There seemed to be a lot the staff weren't saying, and he was more than a little intrigued.

The sun lay low in the sky as he drove up the

winding highway into the leafy Perth hills. Twenty minutes later, he negotiated the steep, dirt driveway that led to TJ's property. Lush wild grass swept the hillside toward the log cabin perched at the top.

A creek meandered past and disappeared through the tall gum trees. Weak sunlight filtered through the smoky haze generated by slow-burning wood heaters that warded off the evening chill in surrounding homes. To the left of the log cabin, several smaller cabins stood empty and crumbling, windows glinting dustily in the dying rays of sunshine.

Scott shivered. It was beautiful, magical and sad all at the same time. He pulled into the gravel clearing that served as the front yard.

He got out of the ute to study the old cabin. Solid jarrah logs made up the walls that rested on a stone foundation, as ramshackle as the rest of the place. The corrugated roof sagged at one end of the veranda where the post had buckled under its weight. The stairs were covered in moss caused by damp from untended guttering. Carefully, he climbed them to the veranda, the slippery, cold stone loose under the soles of his shoes. Brunswick Green paint on the front door peeled away in chunks, revealing a good, solid Jarrah door underneath. Scott raised his hand to knock, but paused as he heard his name.

'Well, Scott bloody *Professional Spotlight* Devin put paid to that idea now, didn't he?' There was no heat in the words, only annoyance tinged with a taste of hopelessness.

'You have to sell, before it's too late,' a male voice replied.

'No way. I've put far too much work into planning the refuge already.'

'You have to give up on this crazy idea that you can save the bloody world from drugs and violence. Before it kills *you*, TJ.'

'It's not a crazy idea. At least I have the guts to try, and I *won't* give up on those kids. Could you? They need somewhere to go, Rob. Somewhere they feel safe, secure, and comfortable off the streets. Surely there's another way?'

'There is no other way, and you know it. For God's sake, TJ, the bank is threatening to foreclose on the mortgage, the council has imposed expensive restrictions on the removal of the asbestos, and the builders have refused to do the work because of the location. Your fundraising efforts have fallen in a heap because the community doesn't want the project to go ahead. They're terrified they're going to have delinquent teenagers running riot in the hills. Oh, and did I mention you're out of a job? You are *never* going to get this off the ground. If you sell now, you'll at least have money to fix Sheila and keep Bruce. There won't even be enough left over to buy somewhere else.' Frustration gave way to concern. 'You *have* to stop thinking about those kids and think about yourself for a minute.'

'You know I won't give up on them. Anyway, where would I go? This is the only home we've ever known. Pop left the house to me. I owe it to him to rebuild his dream. I promised. He provided a home for us when Mum died. His dream was to provide that refuge to others too, and I won't let him down.'

'You're *broke*. I'm not sure it's your choice to make anymore. You could come and stay at my place, I guess.' Resignation rang in his voice, a man willing to accept his fate.

TJ's laugh rang out across the hill and sent pleasant tingles down Scott's spine as he listened. 'We'd kill each other. Besides, you have only one bedroom.'

'It wouldn't be the first time we've bunked together.'

That was it. He'd heard enough. Scott stepped around the corner onto the wooden slats of the veranda. They creaked under foot. TJ and the man turned their heads. They sat close together, each with a beer in hand. Perched on the thick, wooden veranda railing, they sat facing the view with the creek tinkling past below them.

Slowly, TJ swung her legs across the railing and jumped down to the wooden deck. She perched her beer bottle in the spot her bum had vacated and wiped her hands on her denim shorts. 'You're trespassing, Mr Devin.'

'TJ, don't be rude.' Her companion gave her arm a light punch.

Scott tried hard to focus on her attitude and not look at her long, sun-kissed legs in well-worn denim shorts. Ragged around the edges and faded in all the right spots, they fit snugly. Her cotton shirt was secured with a knot above her navel, exposing a hint of creamy skin. Yep, trouble with a capital T. 'I thought I'd stop by with your tool box key. Tony's a little busy.'

'No shit.' She folded her arms and tapped her foot impatiently. 'That might be because he's a pair of hands short.'

'Could be. Which is the other reason I'm here.' Scott shrugged and looked past her to the man standing beside her. He extended his hand, nodding as Rob shook it.

'Please excuse my sister's bad manners. I'm Rob Stevens.'

'Scott bloody *Professional Spotlight* Devin.'

Rob grinned and nudged TJ with his shoulder. 'That's what you get for being a smarty pants.' To Scott he said, 'Can I get you a beer?'

'Thanks. I think I'm going to need it.' Scott grinned back.

'I'll be right back. TJ, behave yourself.' The screen door slammed behind him.

TJ turned her back on Scott and went to lean on the veranda railing. She swept the bottle up, curled her fingers around it and raised it to her lips. 'You could have saved yourself the trouble and called me instead. Or got HR to post it to me.'

He moved to stand next to her. Hands flat on the railing, he followed her stare across the valley and down to the creek. 'I could have done that, yes. Look, I know we got off on the wrong foot yesterday. I apologise for that. I've had a chat to Tony about the workshop. I'd like to offer you your job back.'

'No thanks. I'm sure something else will come up.'

'The team's threatened to down tools until you come back.'

'They won't do that.'

'I had four resignations yesterday.'

TJ's reply was to take another swig of her beer. He watched as she lowered the bottle and picked at the label until it began to peel away.

'Tony says you may have some answers for me about the business,' he tried again.

'Depends on the questions.'

Scott raked a hand through his hair. She wasn't going to make this easy. He should walk away now. Employees had challenged him before, and he hadn't let them get away with it. Why was he giving TJ so much rope? With anyone else, he would have sent them on their way.

'Look, perhaps I was a bit hasty in firing you. I'm sorry. I checked the safety records and they're impeccable. I can see you take safety seriously.'

The mocking look she cast sideways suggested he should have checked those first. 'Before firing me would have been nice.' She pushed away from the railing and paced the deck.

'Will you at least think about it?' He turned to watch her, leaning his hip against the railing.

She stopped pacing and stared at him. Green eyes narrowed on blue before travelling across his face. 'Probably not, but now I know where I've seen you before.'

The change of subject threw him momentarily. He frowned as he straightened. *Professional Spotlight?'*

'No. Sprawled across Rose Devin's buffet.'

He laughed out loud. 'As … decadent … as that sounds, I'm sure you're referring to Mum's photo collection since she's your neighbour.' He pushed away from the railing and stepped toward her.

'So, you're the son Rose brags about. I've seen you naked.' Her eyes mocked him as she held his and took another swig of her beer.

'I was two.' Clearly, she wasn't going to make this easy for him.

'If the rumours are to be believed, many others have seen you naked since.'

'Does that bother you?'

Her gaze ran the length of him, up from his shoes to his face and down again before she shrugged. 'You're not my type.'

'And you're avoiding answering the questions I came here to ask.'

'My prerogative, Mr Devin. Can I have my toolbox key now?'

'No. I need an answer first. Will you come back?'

'The answer is still the same as it was. No.'

'The whole team will leave.'

'I believe that's your problem, not mine.' Her eyes narrowed on his face.

'Then I keep the key. You have until Monday to think it over.'

'The answer will be the same.'

In two angry strides, he stood in front of her. 'Stop being so damned stubborn. I made a mistake. Your team needs you. And they think you're the next best thing since fried bread because of the miracles they tell me you make happen. They just won't tell me what those miracles are.'

Her eyes glittered angrily. She drew herself to her full height and still didn't reach his chin. What she lacked in height, she made up for in attitude. Her breath came fast, her chest rising and falling, every intake brushing her breasts against his shirt. 'Maybe *you* should have checked how things work and thought them through before you fired me. You have no idea how many lives you've just put on the line because you had a knee-jerk reaction.'

'Then explain it to me.' He reached out to tilt up her

chin, mesmerised by eyes that sparked with indignation. 'On Monday. If you're a no-show, I'll send someone around with your tools.'

TJ stood her ground, hands on her hips, and stared him down until he stepped away and turned around. As he walked away, the burn of her gaze fell hot on his back.

Chapter Three

The loud cheer that raised the roof of the workshop as she sauntered through in her safety boots, made her smile. Cat calls followed her as she made her way to the clock machine. Scott Devin pushed through the door to the workshop just as she drew level with it as if he'd been waiting and watching for her to arrive. Wordlessly, he tossed her toolbox key to her.

She caught it effortlessly, pocketed it, and walked around him to clock in. 'Where's the booking schedule, boys? Who's taking first swing?'

Scott turned on his heel and pushed his way back through the door.

Relieved, TJ blew the stray strands of hair out of her eyes before turning to face the team. She rattled off the job allocations and, one by one, the technicians dispersed.

'Marty?' she called. No response. 'Tony, where's Marty?' Her heartbeat raced.

'Dunno. Trades college?'

'No, college is Tuesdays for him. Anyone seen Marty?'

There was a chorus of 'no' and headshaking.

'Damn it!'

She whipped her phone out of her pocket and dialled. Marty's mum was as unhelpful as usual. She didn't know. The boy was his own boss. TJ tried Marty's phone and swore again as it went to voice mail.

'Damn it, Tony! You were supposed to keep an eye on him.'

'Geez, TJ … do you know how busy we were without you? Besides, he was here on Friday.'

'Why didn't you pick him up for work this morning?'

'Because he said he'd catch the train.'

'You know when he catches the train we always send someone to meet him.' Fear for Marty had her snapping. She willed herself to calm down. Maybe the boy was just running late.

'I'm sorry, TJ. I had no one to send. Short-staffed, remember?'

She punched the number of the railway police into her phone. She had an arrangement with them for all her project kids. The railway police kept an eye on them from the time they boarded until they got off at their home station.

'You guys seen Marty Petrowski today?'

'No, TJ. Problem is, we haven't seen any of the other Tag Raiders either, although we're seeing a fair bit of their artwork around the place this morning. Looks like the boys went on a bit of a spree last night. The freight train to Kalgoorlie copped a tagging on the way out.'

TJ's heart sank to her stomach. That wasn't a good sign. Tags and benders usually went hand-in-hand. She'd spent months working hard to keep the gang off the streets and out of trouble. Four boys — Tiny, Marty, Luke and Connor. Four troubled boys, lost somewhere between boyhood and manhood as they bowed under peer pressure and the lure of drugs and alcohol. If none of them were on the train today, it could mean only one thing. They were back on the streets, looking for trouble.

'*Shit*. Thanks, mate. If you see any of them, tell them to call me.' She hung up. 'Tony, you're in charge. I'm going after Marty.'

'You can't. Not on your own. Remember what happened last time? You almost got yourself killed.'

She shivered. 'I have to find him. I can't have him going off the rails again, especially now with Scott Devin in charge. The whole program is at risk.'

'Then take him with you.'

'Who? The new boss? You can't be serious?'

Tony's look told her he was.

'Well, I guess that would give him a first-hand look at the reason for the apprenticeship rehabilitation program. Or it could be the final nail in the coffin.'

Tony shrugged. 'Or you can wait to see if Marty shows up.'

'You know what this means. He's not going to show up. He thinks I'm not here anymore, so the whole thing will go out the window. Along with everything else we've tried to make this program work. Damn it! Give me the keys for the service ute.'

Tony flicked them off the wall and held them up in the air out of her reach. It was at times like these that being short really sucked.

'You gonna ask the boss to go with you?'

'Yes, damn it. Give me the keys!'

He kept them suspended in the air in one hand and held out the other.

'What?' she snapped.

'That'll be $1 for the swear jar.'

She swore again and fished out $1.20. Slapping the coins into his palm, she jumped up and grabbed the keys out of his other hand. She swung through the connecting door at a run and only stopped when she reached Scott's office door.

Taking a deep breath, she knocked twice and opened

the door without waiting for a response. 'Mr Devin, I need you to come with me.'

'To where? I'm trying to sort through this mess.'

'That mess is nothing compared to the mess you're going to be in if you don't help me find Marty.'

'Is that a threat, Miss Stevens?'

'Not even close. It's a promise. There's no time to explain. Please, I need you to come with me. Right now.'

The urgency in her voice had Scott grabbing his jacket from the back of the chair. 'Trouble?'

'Of the worst kind. Where we're going, you're not going to need a jacket. In fact, leave your watch and any other valuables behind too — including your wallet.'

He raised his eyebrows but dropped the jacket on his desk to remove his watch and roll up his sleeves. 'I guess I don't have a choice but to trust you on this one. Where are we going?'

'To one of the worst places you'll ever need to go. If Marty is where I think he is, he's in big trouble and we need to get to him before it's too late.'

'What kind of trouble?' Long legs carried him across the office. In a flash, he had her by the elbow and gently urged her out the door.

'I'll tell you more on the way.' She ran as he strode beside her to the ute. She barely gave him a chance to open the door before she had it in gear and was pulling away.

'Tiger, we *really* need to talk about safety at the next toolbox meeting.' He sighed as he snapped his seatbelt buckle into the retainer.

She cast him a mocking glance as she pulled into the traffic, one hand on the wheel, the other dialling a number on her mobile.

'Remind me to have Bluetooth fitted to the ute,' he said.

'Great idea.' She put the phone up to her ear. 'Mark, you might want to follow me. I'm heading to the Tag Raiders clubhouse. Yes, I'm talking on hands-free. Here, you can ask my boss.' She tossed the phone into Scott's lap.

He picked it up with a shake of his head. 'Scott Devin.'

'She wasn't on hands-free, was she?' A voice chuckled in his ear.

'Uh, nope.'

'I didn't think so. Are you going with her to the clubhouse?'

'I guess?'

'Good. The last time she went down there, we brought her back in an ambulance. I don't want to have to do that again.'

'Of course not.'

'I'm Detective Mark Johnson. My partner Harold Jones and I will meet you down there. Try to keep her alive until we get there.'

Scott looked over at TJ. She raised her eyes to the roof lining of the cab.

'I can't make any promises.' He hung up on the detective's chuckle. 'Why did you come back in an ambulance?'

'Tiny had a syringe filled with drugs. He aimed, I blocked hard and sprained my wrist. He got me in the leg with the syringe. The good news is that, after months of waiting, I got the all-clear.'

'Tiny?'

'The gang leader and, yes, he is tiny. About my height, thin as a stick and, when he's on meth, as strong as a big red kangaroo.'

Scott gripped the car door handle as she weaved in and out through the traffic. He closed his eyes as she came a little too close to a rear bumper. 'So why are we going down there with the cops on our tail, and why is it messy for me?'

She braked to take the turn onto the highway and accelerated up the ramp to merge with the traffic. 'Because you own the program, and Marty is your responsibility.'

'What program?'

She cast him a glance. 'You don't know about the program? Wasn't it in the business plan?'

'I'm discovering that there are a lot of things that weren't in the business plan.'

'Damn!' She fiddled in the top pocket of her overall

shirt and pulled out 20c. 'Keep that for me. I'm going to be broke before pay day at this rate. We're a flagship dealer for the apprentice rehabilitation program. We take in juvies, give them an apprenticeship, mentor them, train them and attempt to rehabilitate them. While they're in our care, we are their guardians, or try to be. Each one comes with a contract. We lose one, we have to explain it to the judge. They have a counsellor from the apprenticeship board who comes in once a week to monitor and report. He's due in on Wednesday. We need to find Marty and pray that Tiny hasn't got him high again by experimenting with new drugs. If we're too late, we have less than two days to get him cleaned up for inspection.' She took an exit off the highway into an industrial area. 'Tiny was one we lost. He went back on the street. Now he's a nom for Beyond Hell's Reach.'

'Jesus. The bikies? You're messing with some dangerous people here, TJ.' Scott digested the information as she pulled up into the car park of a block of storage units. 'Has Marty fallen off the wagon before?'

'Not in the last six months. The last time was when council slapped a stop-work order on the renovation of the cabins.'

'The ones on your property?'

'Yes. It was supposed to be a weekend building project for the kids to keep them off the street. We had to stop because of the asbestos in the cladding. We need professionals to do the removal because of the health risk. Tiny and Marty ran away. They figured if there was no place for them to stay, the apprenticeship program would be canned too. I got Marty back out of the gang but lost Tiny. These kids don't need a lot of convincing from the bad guys when they think no one good wants them. They just want to belong. Somewhere. Anywhere.' She switched off the ignition and pocketed the keys. 'Stay here. They don't know you, so if they see you, they'll think you're either a cop or mark. But if you see me getting a hiding, feel free to butt in.'

'I'm not letting you go alone.'

He was out the door and standing in front of the car before she could argue. TJ sighed. 'Don't blame me if you take a beating. I hope you know how to stop a knife. You're the reason he ran away. It's unlikely he'll be feeling friendly.'

'That's a chance I'll have to take. He ran away because I fired you?'

'No, he ran away because you put the only thing he has left in jeopardy by firing me. Again.' She moved toward the second warehouse on the block. 'Marty!'

Silence greeted her call. TJ darted between the walls of the storage units, searching left and right as she rounded each corner. Scott followed closely. He slammed into her back as she drew to a sudden halt. His arms wrapped around her waist automatically to stop her falling forward. Her breath whooshed out as she found herself plastered against him. The arms that formed an iron band around her tightened. Warmth flooded her and she closed her eyes, savouring the security of his body, hard and muscular at her back … just for a moment.

'Well, fuck me, TJ. Look at you come back for more. Didn't you learn your lesson last time?'

TJ opened her eyes to see Tiny standing in the gap between the units. As he moved closer, she could see the sheen of sweat on his freckly brow. His pupils were large black masses in his normally muddy brown eyes. Shaky fingers curled around a baseball bat.

TJ wriggled free of Scott's arms, relieved when he let go easily, pleased when he stayed close behind her as she stepped forward.

'Tiny, where's Marty?'

The boy shrugged. 'Dunno, mate. Wish you would just leave us alone.'

TJ wanted to grab him by the ear and give him the damn good shaking he needed. In his current drugged state, it would be a waste of energy. She stepped forward. He raised the bat.

'I know he's here, Tiny. I've come to take him home. There's always room for you too.'

'What do you care? We're just the shit on the streets!' His speech slurred as he staggered and put a hand against the shed wall to steady himself. He blinked the sweat from his eyes.

TJ used the distraction to step forward and make a

grab for the bat. An instant too late, Tiny snapped to attention and wrestled her for it. He pulled it away and brought it down toward her shoulder. It never made contact. All TJ saw was Scott's big hand shoot past her and grab the head of the bat. She felt the force of the connection vibrate through his arm, heard the *thwack* as it hit the flat of his palm. Within seconds, he had Tiny face down in the dirt with his arms pinned behind him and a knee in his back.

'Where's Marty?'

The boy remained stubbornly silent.

'You have three seconds before the cops arrive. Hear those sirens?'

Tiny lifted his head to spit on the ground. 'Means nothing, dude.'

'It should.'

'The cops are useless. A stint in juvie, we get bail posted by the big boys, and we're on the street again. They can't touch us, man!'

'You're not dealing with the cops now. You're dealing with me. And last time I looked, you're in breach of your contract. Hello, I'm your new boss. So, guess what? As soon as the paperwork is signed, you're back in the program.'

'I'm not coming back to that dumbass program to be told what to do by that bitch.' He spat in the dirt again.

'You can and you will. Because, right now, that girl you just called a bitch is the only one looking out for you.' Scott pulled the boy to his feet with a jerk, keeping his arm behind his back. He pushed him forward to where the unmarked police car had come to a halt, blue light flashing on the dashboard. 'Detective Johnson?'

'Yep. Where's TJ?'

'Oh for —' Scott handed Tiny over. 'She was here a second ago. Keep an eye on Tiny for me.'

'Wait, I'll go with you.' Mark took his jacket off and threw it in threw the open window of the car.

They turned in the direction Scott had last seen her go. TJ came running around the corner toward them, her phone to her ear.

As she spoke into the phone, she waved for them to follow her and turned back around. 'I need an ambulance to the storage units at 1059 Industrial Parade. Martin Petrowski, aged 16. A suspected overdose. Possibly cocaine. He's collapsed on the floor and having seizures. The boy has epilepsy. I'll do what I can to help him until the ambulance arrives. Please hurry. The police are already here.' She hung up and led Scott into a pile of large crates stacked together to form a cubby. In the corner lay Marty. His body jerked and shivered as tremors racked it. His feet kicked out wildly.

'I'll grab his legs. Get him on his side so he doesn't choke.' In a flash, Scott was on the floor, dodging Marty's feet and knees. He threw his upper body across the boy's legs and pinned them down. Marty continued to squirm.

'Marty, mate, it's TJ. We're here to help you.' She reached for his face to get him to focus on her. Her words wouldn't make sense to him, but she continued to speak, soothing, comforting. Spit formed around Marty's mouth as he thrust his head from side to side. She reached for his shoulders and forced him onto his side, pinning him there as she started to sing, her voice tight with tears she tried hard to hold back.

'Well, there's a little boy waiting at the counter of a corner shop ...'

By the time she got to the second chorus, the wail of the approaching ambulance accompanied her, and the boy's body had stilled. The only sounds in the makeshift clubhouse were TJ's sweet voice and Marty's shallow breathing.

Chapter Four

Marty disappeared behind the ambulance doors, tightly strapped to the stretcher. It would take him a while to come down and be treated before she could see him. Thank God they'd found him in time. Tears stung her eyes and slid unchecked down TJ's cheeks. How many more times could this happen before she wasn't able to get to him in time? She wiped the tears away with the edge of her shirt. Bone-weary exhaustion dragged at her body and mind as the adrenaline wore off. Too many sleepless nights, roaming the streets, watching out for the boys. How much longer could she keep it up?

Firm hands descended on her shoulders and squeezed gently. 'You okay?'

She nodded, not quite trusting her voice yet. Scott turned her to face him and spotted the tear tracks. He fished out his handkerchief, tipped up her chin and scrubbed them away.

'They're taking Tiny in. I'll be at the hearing to make sure we get him back into the program. We need to talk about this, TJ.'

She nodded again, keeping her gaze trained at a point over his shoulder. The boys had handed him the perfect excuse to can the program. 'Can it wait?' The pain in her voice couldn't be disguised.

'Sure.' Scott tipped up her chin again so that she had no choice but to meet his eyes. 'This afternoon. My office. After lunch. Now give me the keys. I'm driving this time. I'd like to get back to the office in one piece.'

She fished out the keys and dropped them in his outstretched palm. With his hand at her back, she let him guide her to the ute. Silence screamed in the cab as Scott negotiated his way back to the highway. TJ stared out the window, her fingers worrying the hem of her shirt. He leaned over and put his hand on hers, stilling the movement. She jumped at his touch, her nerves stretched beyond breaking point.

He withdrew his hand and concentrated on the road ahead. 'What was the singing about?'

TJ sighed. 'Each kid who comes through the program is given a signature tune. Some songs are assigned through mishaps, others — like Marty's — are earned through habits. When Marty first started with us, he was given all the dirty jobs to do, like emptying bins and cleaning toilets. That's what all first-year apprentices have to do. He became bored quickly and wanted to move on to doing real work. When I handed out the jobs in the mornings, he'd stand in the queue and shout, "What about me, TJ? What about me?" Now every time he says it, we all start singing that song. We all have our own songs. It makes the workshop fun because at any time someone can say or do something that starts up a chorus. It also stopped all the arguing over which radio station should be playing.'

'What's yours?'

'My what?'

'Signature tune.'

She smiled, a melancholic tilt to her mouth. 'Tiny and Marty chose mine. They call me Tiger Jane because when I yell, everyone drops and runs.'

The boys were right. There was a lot more to TJ than he knew. He wouldn't mind finding out, but that was a dangerous game to play. Don't meddle in your own backyard. He'd learnt that lesson after his relationship with Serena Snow.

'So, what song did they choose for you?'

'Helen Reddy's *I am Woman.*'

Scott laughed. 'It suits you. I've heard you roar, Tiger. What about the swear jar?'

'The swear jar is our Christmas fund. Every time you swear, you're fined 20c and it goes into the swear jar. At the end of the year, we divide it up equally and use the proceeds to buy each other Secret Santa gifts.'

As they approached the dealership, silence fell between them. Scott parked the ute in a service bay. Neither made a move to get out. After a few moments, TJ held out her hand for the key.

'We also have drinks at the pub on a Friday night after work. You're welcome to join us.'

'Would I be welcome though? I'm still an outsider.'

'Then Friday drinks would be the best way to shake it off.'

Scott shrugged. 'I guess.' He studied her for a long moment before opening the door. 'My office … 1.30pm. Don't be late.'

TJ stood outside the office door and checked the urge to run a comb through her unruly hair and wipe the grease off her face. She had no need to impress Scott Devin. Even if he had earned brownie points during Marty's rescue, he was still a pompous arse. As long as she continued to think of him as one, she could tame that squishy feeling in her stomach that stirred at the thought of him. He may not be a supporter yet, but he hadn't shown himself to be a total enemy either. That only made him more attractive.

For goodness' sake, what was wrong with her? She spent forty hours a week surrounded by males who had all tried to flirt with her at some point. Never mix business with pleasure. It always ended badly. It was the reason she treated them all like big brothers, keeping to safety in numbers by going out with them in a group and never anywhere else but to the pub on a Friday.

None of them had sparked the instantaneous reaction that Scott Devin had. Perhaps it was those dark, brooding looks. Or those blue eyes that seemed to look into her soul and see the things she kept hidden from the world.

Focus. Butterflies fluttered in her stomach. Focus on the project and the lives of the four boys at stake. So far, Scott had been introduced to only two. TJ knocked on the door and waited for him to answer before entering.

'Take a seat while I finish these off.'

TJ sat and watched his big, strong hand flick the pen through graceful swirls as he signed off on the stack of invoices the admin department had left on his desk. She remembered the warmth as he'd touched his hand to hers in the ute earlier. The strength she'd felt when he'd held her shoulders. The iron band his arms had formed around her waist, his strength at her back. Could she trust that strength to be there for the boys too? Or would they be let down again? She was tired from shouldering the responsibility single-handedly, but she couldn't let them down. On edge, she stood up and began to pace. With a sigh, Scott tossed the pen on the pile of invoices.

'For God's sake, sit down and stop pacing.'

'Can't. I'm too wound up.'

He reclined in his chair and placed his hands behind his head. TJ turned to the window to look across and up to the hills. She'd rather be up there under Bruce's bonnet, working off steam than caged up in an office with a man whose growl matched a Tassie Devil's and probably had a bite to match.

'I'm not going to lie, I don't like what I saw out there today.' His voice rippled up her spine.

'Which part? The part where a boy almost died, or when I had to down tools and take off to find him?' Mal had hated that. He never saw the lives at stake, he only ever saw the dollar amount in his bank account.

'Does it always have to be an argument with you, TJ?'

'Yes.'

'Why?'

'Because those boys' lives are worth *so* much more than a bottom line on a spreadsheet.'

'Do you think I'm going to can the program?'

'After what you saw today? And when you get a good look at the cost? Yes.'

Scott sat up in the chair and turned it toward the window. She turned to lean her hips against the window sill. Sunlight shot fire through her hair as she loosened it from the rubber band. He watched her twist the rubber band around her fingers as her hair fell forward around her shoulders. Conscious of his gaze moving from her hands up to her hair, she quickly gathered it together, twisted it back into a pony tail and secured it. She shoved her hands into her pockets and crossed her booted feet.

He tilted his head to one side. 'Now, why would I do that?'

She shrugged. 'Mal always felt the money we got from the program could be put to better use. He didn't think it should be wasted on rehabilitating juvenile delinquents. He figured as long as we ticked the boxes, it didn't matter what happened to the boys.'

'I'm not Mal Malone.'

'No, you're not. Mal would never have come with me today the way you did. Nor would he have dealt with Tiny the way you did. I have to give you credit for that.'

'Thanks for that.' His tone held a touch of mockery as Scott stood up and walked closer. 'I've looked at the contracts. I've also looked at the cost of the program versus the grant money we get for running it. There's a big discrepancy.'

TJ felt her heart sink. It always came down to money. She stared at her boots so he couldn't see the hurt in her eyes. 'I wouldn't know. But I do know that not a penny was spent on the program.'

'So, I noticed,' he said, drily. 'It looks there was a little clever accounting going on. I'm going to have to get the auditors in. What'll happen to Tiny and Marty after today?'

He stood toe to toe with her and tipped up her chin. His eyes narrowed on hers as tears shimmered. TJ cursed herself for the weakness and a mentally added another 20c to the swear jar. She tipped her head away from his hand and stepped around him, putting some distance between them. Her focus needed to be on the boys. She couldn't fully trust her new boss. Not yet.

'Tiny will go back to juvie and Marty will be released back into the program. I'll have to file a report on Marty and there'll be an investigation by the department.'

'Can I appeal on Tiny's behalf?'

She turned and frowned. 'Why would you?'

'Because he's in breach of contract. Why Mal didn't pursue that line rather than have funding for Tiny pulled, I don't know.'

'Because Tiny, the boy, didn't matter to Mal. There would always be another name to add to the books.' Temper flashed in her eyes, and she let the frustrations of the past months come to the fore. 'What about the next line Tiny and Marty snort? You saw what happened out there today. It's not like they're just smoking the odd joint. Weed is nothing compared to the drugs these boys are taking. And the mix gets more toxic every day.'

'You can't save them all, TJ.' The softness she'd glimpsed in him earlier was gone. The businessman was back.

'No, I can't. But I can damn well try. You've been

here two minutes and already you're only thinking of the bottom line. Like all your predecessors, it's the dollar that counts. You can't measure children's lives in dollars and cents, Mr Devin. I will find another way if I have to and then you can take that grant and shove it squarely up your —'

'God damn it, TJ, get off your bloody high horse.' His eyes flashed on hers, his face just inches away. 'Do you think I don't care about those kids out there? Can you at least give me time to get my head around what needs to be done for them to make the program cost-effective?'

'Get out of my face.' Her voice dropped to a growl.

For the life of him, he couldn't. The intriguing mixed perfume of grease and rose-scented soap teased his senses. He'd let her get under his defences. That was a mistake. He lifted his hand to thumb a tear from her cheek. 'I've made you cry.'

Her eyes sparked fire and her throat worked furiously. 'Please don't pretend you care.'

'Give me a chance to care. All I'm asking is a little time to look into what's going on here.' He cupped her cheek with his hand. 'It's ground zero for me, TJ. There's a lot to process here.'

'Don't let me waste any more of your time then.' She pushed his hand away, turned and walked out the door without looking back.

Chapter Five

Scott shuffled the ever-growing pile of papers on his desk. It had been a long, confusing, energy-draining week. Ever since a certain red Gemini and its owner had blown their way into his life, his concentration levels had been on a permanent rollercoaster.

TJ had ignored him for the rest of the week. The only contact being when the counsellor had arrived to find Marty still in hospital. They'd discussed the consequences of the boy's actions and what could be done in terms of the program. Then she'd gone back to the workshop without a word and had avoided him since.

That was a good thing, right? Or it would be if he wasn't concerned about the strain that showed on her face or the snap he heard in her voice. He hadn't been able to stay away from the workshop and stop himself from checking up on her. He'd found excuses to ask Tony questions or drop money in the swear jar. At this rate, he'd have it filled well before Christmas, which was still six months away.

He'd survived his first week, but God, he was looking forward to a weekend at home with his parents. He hoped he wouldn't run into TJ, given that her property bordered his parents' place.

Scott pinched the bridge of his nose and squeezed his eyes shut. He could feel a headache brewing. Ignoring it, he pushed up out of his chair and collected his jacket and briefcase.

His rented townhouse was cold and empty as he threw a change of clothes and toiletries into an overnight bag. He couldn't wait until he found a place with a garden big enough for Sarge. He missed his dog and the companionship they shared.

What was TJ doing for the weekend? He gave himself a mental shake. It wasn't any of his business and he shouldn't be wondering. Certainly not from a personal perspective. Women were trouble, trouble he didn't need to have again, especially at work.

That was a lesson he'd learned the hard way with Serena. Passionate, driven, ambitious and willing, Serena had once been warm and cuddly … until she had the promotion she wanted. A lucky escape. He had no intention of becoming involved in a personal relationship with an employee again. The consequences were never pretty.

As the sun set behind the hills, he drove up the long gravel driveway of his parents' home. Welcoming lights blinked in the windows. His mother stood at the bottom of the stairs that led from the wraparound veranda to the circular gravel drive.

'Scott, you're home!' She threw her arms around him as soon he stepped out of the car.

He hugged her tightly. 'Hello, Mum. Happy birthday.' The scent of roses tickled his nose again. 'New perfume?'

She nodded. 'A birthday present from TJ. I couldn't be happier that it was you who bought the dealership from that Mal bloke. He was a piece of work. I've invited TJ over for dinner tonight too. I hope you don't mind. She's all alone in that house.'

Scott stiffened slightly and smiled. 'Of course not, Mum. It's your birthday.'

She smiled back. 'I heard you met Sheila. You should get TJ to introduce you to Bruce. Did she tell you that the towing company has refused to tow Sheila up here?'

'No, she didn't. I guess that explains why I had to push that pile of junk into the workshop tonight after a week on the driveway. I'll let her know she can leave the car at the workshop and work on it there.' He leaned back into the car to retrieve his overnight bag. Slinging it over his shoulder and closing the car door, he asked, 'Now have you got any fudge brownies?' Scott hugged his mother and tucked her under his arm as they walked toward the house.

Rose raised a groomed eyebrow at him. Scott had never had much of a sweet tooth. 'Fudge brownies? Are you coming down with something? And don't let TJ hear you calling Sheila a pile of junk.'

Scott laughed. 'I've got a craving. It's been a very long week.'

'You're in luck then. I actually do have some. TJ loves fudge brownies, so I made up a whole batch.'

They entered the warm house and Rose led him to the kitchen where a fresh pot of coffee brewed on the Aga. She poured the coffee into earthenware mugs and handed him one before curling her hands around her own. 'She's a great girl, Scott. A hard worker. I worry about her out here all alone when she has those kids staying over there. Dad and I try to keep an eye out when they're here doing chores and renovating her property.'

'I had a firsthand look at some of the trouble those boys bring on my first day. She mentioned a problem with the council and removal of asbestos.'

'Take your dad some coffee and talk to him about it. He's been trying to help her get through all the red tape. He's down in the shed. Dinner will be ready soon.' Rose smiled and poured another cup.

Scott and his father strolled back from the shed at the bottom of the garden as TJ jogged up the steep drive. Her heart did a little flip at the sight of him. His dark hair had ruffled in the breeze and stubble shadowed his jaw. He'd tucked a navy polo shirt loosely into sinfully well-fitting jeans that hugged his hips and thighs.

She stopped at the edge of the driveway and waited for them. Scott's eyes collided with hers as he and Bill reached the point where the path met the driveway. TJ stepped around him to throw her arms around his father in a hug.

Bill Devin returned it with equal enthusiasm. 'TJ, glad you could make it. Where's the boy?' He kissed her forehead.

'Marty's still in hospital. I'm picking him up in the morning.' She released Bill from the hug and turned to Scott, keeping her tone cool and impersonal. 'Hi.'

'Hi, TJ.' Scott nodded.

Tension lay thick in the cool evening air. Bill looked from one to the other, his eyes thoughtful. 'Now, I don't know what's going on between you, kids, but you two might want to ease up on the chill before we get to the house. Otherwise, Rose will have you both in her interrogation chair before you can sneeze. TJ, did you need me to give you a lift to the hospital tomorrow?'

TJ hooked an arm through Bill's as they walked a little ahead of Scott. 'No, that's okay. I've got Bruce.'

'Aah, Bruce! Has Scott met Bruce?'

'I think Sheila was enough for him, Bill. Bruce might just push him over the edge.'

Bill chuckled. 'Why don't you take him over there after dinner?'

TJ stiffened. 'I'm sure Scott has better things to do.'

'No, he doesn't.' Bill stopped and untangled his arm from hers. 'Here, talk to him about it while I go in and let Rose know that young Marty will be home tomorrow. She'll have to get baking. That boy will eat like an elephant after a few days of hospital food.'

TJ wanted to beg Bill to stay. She didn't want to be alone with Scott. Not now, not ever. She needed to stay angry at him so she wouldn't be disappointed when he decided the program was too high a risk to his business. TJ started to walk toward the house. His hand at her elbow stopped her short as energy zinged up her arm and churned in her stomach.

'Bruce?' Scott asked as she jerked her elbow out of his hand and walked on.

'A 1953 FJ Holden Ute.'

'Really? Where did you find one of those? Plenty of sedans around but the utes are pretty scarce.' He caught up with her easily as she negotiated the path to the house.

'It was Pop's.'

Scott sighed and stopped walking. 'TJ, I want you to know that I haven't written off your program just yet.'

TJ stopped too but didn't look back at him. Instead, she stared at the house, her back ramrod straight. 'Yet? If that's meant to be a reassurance, it's not cutting it, Scott.' She turned to face him. 'I almost lost another boy this week. A child no one gives a shit about, except me. Not even his own mother.' Against the twilight sky, he stood dark and brooding. If he wasn't a threat to everything she worked so hard to protect, she might even find him attractive. 'I can't abandon these kids and I can only protect them by continuing the program. I love my job and my team, but if you're not on board with this, I'll have to start looking for somewhere that can be.'

'I hear you and I see what you've achieved. I'm not saying no, but I have questions I need answered that I never got around to asking this week. Above all, I have to take your safety into account too. Especially with the power that lies behind all this. No one messes with the one percenters and comes out unharmed, TJ. How about we call a truce? At least until Monday when we can sit down together and work it out.' He held out his hand and she studied it for a minute.

'Truce,' she agreed, accepting his handshake.

'So do I get to meet Bruce?'

She hesitated. 'Maybe tomorrow.' The long walk in the dark, and the intimacy of the moonlit night that blanketed the hills would be far too friendly when she couldn't completely trust him yet.

'Tomorrow,' he agreed as they walked into the house. 'Oh, and TJ?'

'Yep?'

'I heard you're having some trouble with getting Sheila towed up here?'

'Yes. The truck won't make the steep driveway with a load.'

'You can leave her at the workshop and do what you need to there.'

'Thank you.' She accepted his peace offering willingly. 'I appreciate that.'

If there was one thing Scott had missed most while he'd lived on the east coast, it was dinner with his parents. There would always be something special about coming home. TJ helped Rose, comfortable in his mother's kitchen, her guard down as she entertained his parents with the details of her first meeting with him.

'And then … he fired me.'

'Scott! You didn't!' Rose cast an indignant look at him.

Scott shrugged. 'Rules are rules.'

He held TJ's chair out for her to sit as she approached the table, her hands full with dishes of food.

As she put them down on the table and sat, her unique perfume drifted past his nose. The scent had become so familiar in just one week. In the workshop, in the corridor to the offices, pretty much everywhere he turned, and now here in his mother's house. Rules were rules, he reminded himself. He needed to remember that and keep his distance. He moved to the opposite side of the table despite the empty chair next to her.

'The boys declared mutiny and I was forced to give her the job back.'

'I'm sure you didn't need too much persuasion,' Bill said. 'TJ has an impeccable record at Mal's Motors.'

'That she does, Dad. But it was the threats I received that swayed my decision,' he teased. 'TJ has friends with dangerous weapons close at hand in their toolboxes. I wasn't game to risk it.'

'Sheila dropped her bumper on his foot, and he was running scared.' TJ handed him the basket of bread rolls and the butter knife across the table.

He took them from her, frowning when she held on to the basket. 'I was not. Wait, how do you know about that?'

'The boys told me.' Her eyes glittered with laughter as she caught his scowl. She let the basket go. 'Thank you for putting her away in the workshop tonight.'

He shrugged. 'No point leaving her to the mercy of the car yard vandals over the weekend.'

'So, you do care.' Across the table, their eyes met

and lingered. TJ dropped her gaze first and tucked enthusiastically into Rose's tender lamb roast, drizzled with fresh mint sauce.

'When is Sarge coming over, Scott?' Bill broke into the suddenly awkward silence.

Scott thought of his Rottweiler, a 60kg teddy bear that occasionally masqueraded as a guard dog.

'He's staying with a friend of mine until I find a house with a yard big enough for him. The townhouse garden is way too small for him.'

'He can stay here until you find something.' Rose was quick to offer. 'He'd love the open space.'

'Never thought of that, Mum. Good idea. I'll arrange it.'

The conversation moved to house hunting and Scott watched as TJ began to relax again. Dinner passed pleasantly as silence settled in the hills.

'Scott, will you walk TJ home,' Rose asked later as they relaxed over coffee around the fire in the lounge room.

'There's no need. I'll be fine.' TJ's protest fell on deaf ears.

'I know Bill and I normally walk you, but my hip's been playing up.'

Scott's eyes narrowed. Was his mother matchmaking? He hoped not. He shook his head at the exaggeration of her limp as she stood up from the chair.

'Really, Rose. I can look after myself,' TJ argued.

'Now, you know it's so dark out there, you can't see your hand in front of your face with no street lights. I'm sure Scott won't mind.'

Scott did mind. The two of them alone in the dark? Did rules apply in the dark? But his parents were right. Even in an area this safe, no one could take risks.

'I don't mind.' *Liar!* 'If we go now, I can have a look at Bruce.'

TJ hesitated, but the chorus of agreement drowned out any refusal she could make. So, she shrugged and gave in. 'Okay. I'll just help Rose clean up the kitchen and then we can go.'

'No, no. Bill will give me a hand to clean up.' Rose cut off Bill's protest with a silencing look. 'Off you go.'

'Come on, TJ. You won't win this round.'

Scott offered her a hand up out of the bean bag next to the fire. She ignored it and stood up to place her mug on the coffee table. He put both his hands in his pockets. All he needed to do was keep them there. Easy right?

'Thanks for dinner.' She bent and kissed first Rose's then Bill's cheek before heading for the door. 'Night.'

Scott picked up a torch from the hall table and followed behind her, careful not to follow too closely. He put out a hand as she skidded on loose gravel, but she righted herself, clearly drawing the line.

All the way up her steep driveway, he had a view snug denim and her pony tail swinging against the sheepskin jacket that warmed her back. As she veered off the driveway toward a massive shed, he tried to remember the invisible line … and the rules. He liked her fire, her humour, her all-in view of the world, the whole package that was Tiffany-Jane Stevens. But he couldn't let that blur his judgement when it came to deciding what would be best for his business.

She dragged the heavy door back on its sliding groove and snapped on the light. Industrial lighting blinded him momentarily as it revealed a beautifully restored 1953 Holden FJ utility.

'Meet Bruce, the love of Sheila's life,' TJ said waving her hand.

Bruce and Sheila. He shook his head as he watched her snag a polish cloth off the work bench nearby and rub at the chrome badge on the bonnet. Scott stepped up to run a hand over the smooth cream fender before strolling around to admire the rear.

'New look tail light lens, original name badge, original hubcaps. Are these *real* whitewalls?' He moved around the car. 'Modified grille, genuine leather upholstery…' he noted in awe. 'Where did you get all this stuff?'

'… Straight-six grey motor with modified, longer-life pistons and torsional-type compression rings,' she finished for him. 'I worked a lot of extra hours to pay for those parts.'

'Do you plan to do the same for Sheila?' He paused

with his hand on the polished chrome door handle to look at her as she leaned a hip against the work bench.

'Yes.' She hooked the key off a nail above the work bench and tossed it to him. 'Start him up.'

Scott didn't need a second invitation. He caught the key neatly and opened the door to slide in behind the wheel as TJ popped the bonnet. He turned the key and the motor purred to life. He got out and stood next to her.

'Purrs like a kitten.' He ducked his head under the bonnet and turned an ear closer to catch the sound. 'Smooth as silk.'

TJ beamed. 'Hours of fine tuning and good grade oil.'

'You know your stuff,' he said.

He straightened and their shoulders touched. She'd crawled right in under his defences, this enigma that was TJ Stevens, a puzzle he could spend hours trying to solve. Her lack of self-awareness, her energy and enthusiasm, and the fierce pride that came to the fore when challenged … all these traits stirred his senses. He raised his hand to brush a speck of grease from her cheek. She stepped out of reach.

'Mind your hands, Scott. I'll drop the bonnet.'

He folded his arms and leaned against the ute. 'So, tell me about Sheila.'

'Sheila was meant to be a restoration project for the

boys on the program. I supplied the parts, and they would provide the labour.'

'What happened?'

'I ran out of money. I had money saved up for the parts but then I had to use it to apply for the building permit for the restoration of the cabins. Every building inspection cost me and, ultimately, the permit was denied because the asbestos couldn't be removed safely. So, the money reserved for Sheila and the project went down with the plans for the youth camp.'

'What about the grant?'

'It only applies to the apprenticeship program at Mal's Motors. Unfortunately, an apprenticeship will only keep them off the streets during the day.'

'How's that your problem?'

She sighed and walked to the workbench where she played with the array of screwdrivers that lay forgotten on the surface. Slowly, as if measuring her response, she began to place each screwdriver in the allotted rack on the wall. She stretched to reach the top rack, revealing creamy skin as her shirt lifted with each movement.

The bright orange safety step landed with a thump next to her as Scott moved closer. 'Stand on that.'

She stepped onto it and continued her task. 'It's my problem because I chose to make it so. Some of those kids are homeless. They've either been kicked out or run away. Or their parents have simply given up and don't care whether they come home or not anymore. Like Marty.'

'So, you thought you'd build a refuge?'

'Yes. A place where they could sleep, eat and maybe find a purpose in life. I figured if I kept them busy working on cars and around the property, they would learn skills and have a roof over their heads. Maybe even keep them off the streets.'

'And the funding to run it?'

She shrugged. 'I had some charities interested in helping with funding because their own refuges were overflowing. I planned fundraisers and grant applications. Ethan Wright, the program counsellor, was helping me with those.'

'And?'

'It all fell to pieces. The council refused the application because there was some concern that the kids would present a threat to the safety of the community and the security of the area. Until I can prove they won't, the deal's off.'

'So, unless you can secure funding, rebuild the cabins and persuade the boys to stay clean, you're screwed?'

'Pretty much.' She turned on the square step to face him, her eyes now level with his. 'And every day I watch kids like Marty, Tiny, Connor and Luke slip farther away. All I can do is keep trying to get them back.'

'Why?'

'Because someone has to be there for them.'

She held his gaze for what seemed like a lifetime. He felt the impact all the way to his stomach, leaving him in no doubt of how strongly she felt about her lost boys. His hands enclosed her waist, as he lifted her off the step. They stood close for a while before he dropped his hands and stepped back.

'I'll see you to your door. Tomorrow, we'll go to the hospital together to pick up Marty. On two conditions.'

TJ smoothed her shirt down where it had bunched up when he'd lifted her off the step. 'Name them.'

'We take Bruce, and I drive.'

Chapter Six

Deciding what to wear shouldn't be this hard. Discarding her fifth outfit, TJ stood in her underwear and faced her jumbled wardrobe. She was going to the hospital, for God's sake, not on a date. She pulled on her well-worn jeans and partnered them with a long teal singlet under a pink-checked shirt. She tugged on her running shoes and secured her hair in a knot.

She and Scott had made a silent pact over Bruce's fender last night, but she refused to see that as a step toward friendship. If she kept it professional, she wouldn't end up a casualty in the trail he left in his wake. The gossip columns were littered with his cast-offs and, as much as she didn't put much store into gossip, where there was smoke there was usually fire.

She finished tying her shoelaces as he pounded on the door.

'Coming!' She swept through the house and picked up her handbag off the table before whipping the door open. 'Hi.'

Scott stood on her veranda with his sunglasses pushed to the top of his head, looking like temptation. A tight-fitting black T-shirt emphasised every muscle, outlined every contour and clung with the loving affection of well-worn cotton to his chest. He still hadn't shaved. Stubble caressed his jaw, a sinful invitation to wanton fingers to follow the path to equally sinful lips. Just as well she couldn't be tempted.

'Ready?' Even his voice took on the dark slide of velvet. He turned and strode down the steps with a confidence that drew her eyes to the black denim that hugged his hips.

'Ah … bugger!' TJ committed $2.00 to the swear jar. She might as well be in credit.

He opened the sliding door to the shed and TJ had to admit she enjoyed watching the muscles ripple in his arms and across his shoulders. No harm in doing a little window shopping when she had no intention to sample the goods.

'Are you coming or are you going to stand there all day?'

She followed him into the shed, snagging Bruce's

key from the hook as she passed. He held out his hand and she hesitated.

'A deal is a deal,' he reminded her.

She dropped the keys and opened the passenger door. 'He's temperamental.'

'I wouldn't expect otherwise.' He slid in behind the wheel and took a moment to caress the dashboard, outline the gauges and finishes with his fingers.

TJ busied herself with clipping her seatbelt into place. 'You can stroke his dash as much as you like, it won't make him behave any better. Don't say I didn't warn you.'

'Jealous, Tiger?' One hand on the steering wheel, he cast her a sidelong look as he slipped his sunglasses on with the other.

'Hell no. Go ahead and make love to my car's dashboard as much as you like.'

He chuckled as he turned the key in the ignition and the engine roared to life. With expert hands, he guided the old car down the steep drive and Bruce, bless him, didn't slip, stall or sputter once.

'Bloody traitor, Bruce,' TJ muttered.

Scott flashed a grin at her.

They drove in silence as Scott negotiated the winding bends through the hills and down to the flatlands. The boyish grin on his face was contagious, and TJ relaxed a little. Scott Devin didn't have to be driving her to the hospital to pick up Marty. He'd chosen to. He hadn't written her boys off yet. Mal would absolutely not have gone to Marty's rescue the way Scott was doing today. Maybe he wasn't such a bad guy after all.

'So, what happens to Marty when he's discharged?' Scott stopped at the traffic lights that connected them to the highway into Perth.

'I take him home, clean him up, and we start again.'

'How long does he stay with you?'

'As long as he likes.'

'How does he behave after one of these benders?'

TJ stared out the window at the traffic that lined the highway. She clutched the strap of the seatbelt where it crossed her shoulder, her knuckles white. 'It depends on how long he's been in hospital. If whatever he's taken is completely out of his system, he's usually tired and drained. He sleeps a lot and then eats like a horse. If it's not out of his system, he can be difficult, moody, aggressive or worse … suicidal.'

'Jesus, TJ! And you're alone with this kid?'

'Not always. Ethan visits him twice a week, and your mum and dad pop over to make sure everything's okay. My brother Rob comes by after work sometimes and spends time with him.'

'And when they all go home?'

'I'm alone with the kid.' She shrugged. 'Marty won't hurt me.'

'But Tiny would?'

'Tiny only stays with me if Ethan or Rob stay too.'

Scott's mouth was grim. 'So … Ethan?'

'What about him?'

'Are you …?'

'Involved with him? No. Ethan is married to his job. We have an agreement when it comes to the program, that's all.'

'Have you ever been involved with him?'

'We went out on a couple of dates once, but we're friends. Why?'

Scott negotiated the traffic in silence for a moment before replying, 'Just curious about the dynamics of relationships that might affect the boys. Has Marty ever tried to hurt you?'

She remained silent.

'For God's sake, TJ.'

She sighed. 'Once, maybe twice. He has frequent nightmares, hallucinations sometimes, and if he's not fully awake, he can get confused.'

He swore long and hard. 'Why? Why do you put yourself in danger for these kids?'

'Like I've said before, someone has to. I can't do nothing while the monsters behind this ruin these kids' lives.'

'That's what the goddam authorities are for. Where do they fit in?' The flat of his palm smacked against Bruce's steering wheel.

TJ's temper boiled. 'Nowhere, because no one

higher up really gives a flying fuck about these kids.' She stopped, breathed to control the anger and helplessness that came with the battle to save the boys. 'Once they're released to their guardians, they get buried in red tape. The department doesn't have the resources to follow up on every case regularly and sometimes the kids slip through the cracks, especially the older ones. Ethan works for the apprenticeship board, not child protection, but he does what he can with the authority he has.'

Scott reached across to stroke her white knuckles with his thumb. 'I'm sorry.' He squeezed her hand before returning his to the steering wheel. 'When my dog arrives, he's staying with you.'

TJ laughed. 'To do what? Lick them to death? You said yourself he's a teddy bear.'

Scott smiled back. 'Oh, I think he has the heart of a lion if he's forced into it.' He pulled into the hospital parking lot. 'Let's go and see what kind of mood Marty's in. I might have to stay over at your place tonight.'

TJ wasn't sure who she should be more scared of … Marty, Scott or herself. Right now, she wanted to kiss him for being there and taking the situation seriously.

Ethan Wright leaned against the door frame of Marty's room as Scott and TJ walked to the ward. In the stark white light, his face was grim.

'I don't like that look, Ethan.' TJ stopped in front of him and placed a hand on his arm.

He patted her hand and straightened. 'You're not going to like what I have to tell you either.' He leaned down and kissed her cheek before extending a hand to shake Scott's. 'Do you want to see Marty first or should we get business out of the way now?'

TJ sighed. As choices went, neither looked promising. 'Let's get business out the way first. Marty won't mind waiting a little longer. Have you seen him?'

Ethan nodded as he placed a hand in the small of her back to guide her into the visitor's lounge. 'This was a bad round for him. The apprenticeship board has decided to give him one last chance. It took some persuading.'

'Thank you. You know I appreciate how hard you fight. What about Tiny?'

Ethan dropped his hand and shook his head. 'He's off the program. I couldn't change their minds this time. He's eighteen next week and doesn't need parental or guardian consent after that. The board doesn't see him staying of his own free will.'

'So that's it for him?' TJ shuddered at the thought of the consequences of Tiny being homeless, jobless, alone and at the mercy of the streets.

'I'm afraid so ... unless he has a change of heart and toes the line.'

'He can't do that on his own.'

'And you can't put yourself at risk to help him. You've tried. It almost got you killed twice. This is one battle where you're going to have to admit defeat.'

'Defeat isn't a word in my dictionary. You know that.' She folded her arms tightly against her chest. 'I'll find a way.'

Scott moved to join the conversation, two cups of coffee in hand. He offered one to TJ, but she shook her head, so he handed it to Ethan instead. 'What if I get him to sign a workplace contract and take him on as a Trade Assistant?'

'You'd do that? After all the trouble he's caused?' Ethan tipped his coffee cup in a salute. 'I thought you'd put him in the too-hard basket. If he was a cat he'd have used all his lives.'

Scott shrugged. 'It's worth a try. There'd be strict conditions, of course. And he'd be answerable to me, not TJ.'

'You won't receive funding for him. And you'd have to make sure you get to him before he's released. Once he's out on the street again, he's gone for good this time. Beyond Hell's Reach will make sure of it.'

'I'll talk to the judge. Perhaps we can make it part of his conditions for release.'

Ethan shrugged. 'Attending the program was a condition of his release last time, and it made no difference.'

'This time he'll be answering to me.'

TJ listened to the interchange with a flare of hope in her heart. She hoped Scott was serious. There was only one little problem.

'He has nowhere to live. How are you going to make sure he shows up every day?' she interrupted.

'Part of his new contract will be that he lives and travels to work with me. I'll work out the finer details with the judge.'

'And if he falls off the wagon?'

'Between us we have to make sure that doesn't happen. I'll make an appointment with the judge tomorrow and see what we can do. Happy with that, TJ?'

'Thank you.' She wanted to hug him, kiss him even, as a glow of hope shimmered on Tiny's horizon. Instead, she held out a hand. 'It's a deal.'

Her hand disappeared in his firm grip, but he didn't shake it. He pulled her to his side and held on. 'Let's take Marty home.'

Marty was solemn as they signed the discharge papers and led him to the car. The sight of Bruce glinting in the sunlight lifted his spirits.

'Awesome! You brought Bruce. You get the middle seat, TJ. Your legs are shorter'n mine.'

'And if I'm driving?' she teased.

He grinned. 'Guess the boss is drivin' then. 'Cos I

don't see him sittin' in the middle either.'

Scott tossed the boy's battered bag in the back of the ute and dangled the keys. 'I've driven with TJ. I need to top up my insurance before I let her drive me again.' He unlocked the driver's door and slid behind the wheel to reach over and flip up the latch on the passenger side. 'Get in.'

TJ scooted across to the middle, careful not to touch any part of Scott's body. Marty nudged her with his hip.

'You gotta move up, TJ. I can't shut the door.'

And so, she ended up wedged against Scott, shoulder to shoulder, thigh to thigh, thankful that Bruce had column gearshift, not floor shift. She felt each movement of his leg on the clutch, each slide of his arm as he changed gear, and the squeeze of each tight corner he took. The grin on his face said he was enjoying every minute of her awkward discomfort as she tensed up on another roll around a corner. Her spirits lifted a little knowing he wasn't always the serious businessman. Maybe he was what they needed after all, and everything would be okay.

'Hey, TJ. Does my mum know I'm coming home?' Marty broke the silence.

TJ's heart sank. 'I rang your mum this morning. She told me to collect your things. You'll have to stay with me for a while.'

'She's thrown me out?'

'Yes.'

Marty swore and looked out the window. No one held out a hand for swear jar money. TJ patted his hand where it lay against his thigh. He pulled it away and nodded.

'I guess I had that coming, didn't I?' His voice was tight in his throat.

'You'll be okay, Marty. We'll work it out.'

'Sure.' The single word rang with defeat.

Scott placed his sunnies on his head and looked down at TJ. She met his look and fought back the sting of tears. His smile stopped her heart.

'We'll work it out,' he said.

They pulled into the drive and Marty was out the car before the engine had stopped running. He ran around the side of the house and disappeared. Scott made to give chase, but TJ held him back.

'Leave him. He won't run away. He's gone down to the creek. I'll go after him in a while.'

Scott wasn't so sure. 'How do you know he won't make a run for it?'

'It's his favourite spot. When he needs to chill, he goes down there. I can keep an eye on him from the veranda. Rose will be over soon to lure him back with fudge brownies.'

'So, his mum kicked him out?' He pulled Marty's bag out of the back of the ute and followed TJ up the stairs to the veranda.

'Yes. It's a long and sad story of a broken family

who've spiralled out of control. His older brother is in jail for armed robbery, his stepfather is up on charges of abuse, and Marty's mum has five little ones to raise single-handedly. It's not a pretty story.'

'Any hope she'll change her mind?'

TJ shook her head. 'Not this time. Want a beer?'

'Sounds like a plan.'

She disappeared through the sliding door into the kitchen and came back moments later with two bottles placed snugly in stubby holders. She handed him one and clinked her bottle against his.

'Cheers!' She hopped up on the railing and swung her legs over the other side to face the creek. Her eyes followed the gentle flow of water until she spotted Marty's dark head leaning against the bark of an old gum tree, skipping pebbles across the stream.

Scott moved to sit next to her on the railing.

'Did you mean what you said about Tiny,' she asked after a few moments of silence.

'Yes. I never say anything I don't mean.'

'What about the cost?'

'The books are a mess. I've asked for an audit so we can set them straight. The grant money wasn't going where it should've. But you knew that.'

'Yes, I knew that.'

'So, now that I've had time to get my head around the true state the business is in, I can start to allocate funds where they need to go. The rehabilitation program has been allocated additional funds over and above the grant.'

TJ played with the label on her bottle. 'Thank you.'

'Oh, it comes with a price.'

'Doesn't everything in life?'

'Once a week, we have a meeting with everyone on the program, yourself and Tony included, so we can deal with any problems as a team. Any trouble, I want to know about it immediately. We'll work on developing a reward system to keep them interested and motivated. No, don't thank me yet …' He held up a hand to stop her as she opened her mouth to speak. 'Every Friday, I want a written progress report, which you and I will discuss and determine any action that needs to be taken. Deal?'

She held out her hand. 'Deal.' It was hard to stop smiling.

'You have a beautiful smile.' He took her hand and raised it to his lips where he brushed a kiss across her knuckles.

For a moment, she stared into his eyes, dark blue and challenging. She pulled her hand from his grip slowly. 'I'll go see how Marty's doing.' She put down her beer bottle on the railing and jumped the short distance onto the soft grass below, sleek as a cat, and walked away.

Chapter Seven

Monday was shaping up to be a good day. TJ watched Tiny torque the spark plugs on the V8 engine and made a note on her clipboard. On a high, the youngster was a wild, uncontrollable beast. Drug-free, he was little more than a boy, lost and out of control in the vortex of life.

She'd had a hard time putting her concerns aside after Scott's visit, but this morning, back at the workshop where the two boys worked together, she had to admit he might have a point. Having someone share the responsibility for Tiny was definitely a plus.

'Did you clean the debris out of the holes?'

He nodded. 'Now I torque 'em finger-tight, then a half-turn with the wrench.'

'Good work.'

They'd had a smooth two weeks since Tiny and

Marty's release. So far, the boys had toed the line. TJ hoped it would last. Tiny's resentment toward having a girl for a team leader was held at bay by the stern warning from Scott and strengthened by his random visits to the workshop to check up on the youth's progress.

'So, are you and Marty going to give me a hand to fix Sheila tomorrow?'

'I guess.' Tiny shrugged. 'But I gotta cut the lawn out on the front verge first, the boss said.'

'That's cool. Want a lift in?'

'Nah. Comin' in with Mr D.' His head dipped deeper into the engine bay as he tested the torque of the plugs.

'Okay. Are you staying for the barbeque tonight after work?'

'I guess.' Another shrug.

TJ sighed inwardly. Talking to teenagers was like pulling teeth. But at least he was talking. 'I'll go and hand in the weekly report then. Pack it up when you're done and clean up the bay.'

'Sure thing,' he said without looking up as she walked away.

Scott's door stood ajar. TJ took a deep breath and knocked. These weekly progress meetings with him always put her on edge. Things were running too smoothly. She should be happy about that, but the niggle in her belly and past experience had taught her to listen to her gut. Her gut told her the peace wouldn't last. At any point in the program, Scott could still change his mind.

'Come in, TJ. Your timing is perfect. Have a seat.' He waved her over. 'I received the first financial audit report today. Now we can start getting this place back on its feet. We need to discuss action plans.'

'We used to have a quality improvement team. Did you want me to round them up? Or what's left of them.'

The team dedicated to improvement had disbanded when Mr Malone decided it was a waste of resources. The result had sent the customer satisfaction levels plummeting, and the profits along with it.

'Not right away. There are a few things we can deal with first to set the foundation. That's a job for Monday.' He gestured toward the clipboard in her hand. 'Is that Tiny's weekly report?'

'Yep.' The knot in her stomach clenched tighter as his eyes lingered on the clipboard she now clutched to her chest.

'How's he doing this week?'

'Better.' She smiled. 'It feels like we've made progress.' The knot eased a little as she realised Tiny had turned a corner. He was communicating now, even smiling more.

'Let's hope so.' He wiggled his fingers, and she handed over the report. He scanned the first page, taking his time to read the details. 'A definite improvement on last week.'

'How's he going at home?' Nerves had her twisting the edge of her shirt around her fingers. If Scott couldn't cope with Tiny, she didn't know what she'd do.

Scott sat back in his chair as he tossed the clipboard on the desk. 'It's like talking to a brick wall. One-word answers and a lot of grunting. But he doesn't seem too unhappy with the set up. He eats like a horse. How's Marty doing?'

TJ shrugged. 'About the same. He tried to see his mum yesterday, to apologise, but she closed the door on him.'

'That would've hurt. How did he take it?' He leaned forward to place his elbows on the desk, his gaze intense as he focused it on her.

The feeling of a deer caught in the headlights returned. So much depended on how the boys reacted and behaved. One slip and it could all go to hell in a handbasket again. 'He locked himself in his room. I tried to call her, but she didn't answer. This time there really is no going back for him.'

Scott stood to walk around the desk. 'So, he'll stay with you?'

TJ swallowed. The man moved with all the sleekness of a panther, a dangerously attractive trait. He leaned against the desk next to her chair, the material of his black jeans pulled taught across his thighs. She'd always been a sucker for strong thighs encased in denim. Scott Devin was built for loving. Heat rose in her cheeks as she forced her attention back to his question. 'Yes, for however long it takes. I won't abandon him too.'

'You let me know if he gives you any trouble, okay? We're in this together now.' Scott checked his watch before placing his hand on his thigh. 'Is that barbeque on yet?'

Her gaze hitched on his long fingers as they spread across the denim. 'Marty was getting it ready while the other boys cleaned up the shop. Is it okay if we work on Sheila tomorrow?' As she raised her eyes to meet his, she prayed he couldn't read what was going through her mind right now.

'Sure. I'll be here getting ready for the stock audit. What time did you want Tiny here?'

The twitch of those delectable lips suggested he knew exactly where her mind was. It didn't look like he minded a bit either. 'About 8am?'

'Done. Shall we go and have a beer?' He pushed away from the desk, bringing him close enough to touch.

Dear God, she needed one. Her throat was as dry as a week-old bone. Standing up as he moved to the door, she shoved her hands in her pockets. 'Sounds good.'

The barbeque took place on the last Friday of every month in the yard behind the workshop — their reward for the team's hard work. Sausages sizzled on the cast iron grid, filling the air with the mouth-watering aroma of spices as Marty stirred onions next to them. Cold beer lounged amidst bags of ice in the cooler, chequered with cans of cola for the non-drinkers. TJ made her rounds, chatting easily to the staff while keeping a close eye on the apprentices to make sure they didn't sneak a beer behind her back. She noticed Scott doing the same. He stood listening earnestly to the group of administration girls who'd pinned him into a corner.

TJ smiled. *Let that be a lesson to you.* She could only imagine the litany of administrative issues he was being subjected to right now. His eyes caught hers over their heads and he smiled, tipping his beer bottle in a salute. Her heart sped up as she felt the impact of his gaze as surely as if she'd stuck her finger in a power socket. That had to stop.

The jangling of the mobile phone in her top pocket broke the spell. She pulled it out and dropped her eyes to the screen. Another smile flickered on her lips.

'Rob! Where've you been hiding?' The sound of her brother's voice was a welcome distraction.

'Here and there. How's Scott bloody *Professional Spotlight* Devin doing?'

TJ laughed. 'Yeah, he's doing okay, I guess.'

'And the boys? I heard you had a bit of trouble.'

'Nothing we couldn't handle.' She filled him in on the events.

'Wow, that's a big step in the right direction. At least Scott's taking an interest in the program.'

'I guess.' She stepped away from the crowd and wandered down to stand against the back fence of the car yard. 'Any luck with getting the bank to change their minds about the mortgage?'

'I've managed to put their minds at rest about your job situation being stable. They can see the possibilities of increasing the property value by finishing off the buildings but aren't prepared to extend the loan to finance it. Not even if I stand surety for you.'

The joy she'd felt at hearing his voice wilted. 'Damn them for not making it easy!'

'They know about council denying the plans, so that would influence the decision. You can't raise the property value if you don't have building approval.'

'Between a rock and a hard place.' Frustration rode high as she bit out the words. She twisted her ponytail around her index finger.

'Pretty much, little sister. How's Sheila doing?'

'The boys and I are starting work on her tomorrow.' She unravelled her finger from the knot she'd created and flicked her ponytail back over her shoulder. 'At least I can buy the engine parts on my account. The boys down at the engineering shop are going to skim the cylinder head for free. They reckon they owe me a favour.' There were times when her profession and passion definitely came in handy.

'Want me to come down and give you a hand?'

TJ laughed. 'What? And get those pretty calculator fingers dirty?'

'Hey! Those calculator fingers keep your accounts in order, young lady.'

Rob feigned insult, but TJ could hear the smile in his voice. 'You can stop by and say hi, if you like,' she negotiated.

'I might do that. Check out the great Scott Devin in his own environment. And speaking of environments …'

'Uh oh! You've been sniffing around again, haven't you?' Rob believed in researching everything. How many times had she teased him that it was becoming an obsession?

'Yes, and I won't apologise for it either. I have a sister to protect.'

'I think you'll find your sister can protect herself.' TJ rolled her eyes.

'I don't doubt that for a minute, but still … humour me. Your Mr Devin has quite a reputation when it comes to women. It seems there was a little scandal involving a young employee named Serena Snow.'

'Rob, in the working world there are always scandals, real or imagined. This industry has a special reputation for it. You know that. And he's not *my* Mr Devin! Besides, what can you tell me that the gossip columns haven't already made public?'

'That it went to court and got ugly. So ugly that

Scott Devin left town. Hence his interest in a struggling, semi-rural dealership on the opposite side of the country.'

TJ sighed. 'All that means is that he took the opportunity to get out of the spotlight.' She folded her left arm across her chest and rested her hand in the crook of the arm holding the phone to her ear.

'Yes, but it was the reason for the court case that worries me.'

TJ stalked the fence line. 'What was it?'

'I'll swing by this weekend and tell you over a beer. It's a fairly long story. And I want to check him out again for myself first. Sunday lunch at yours?'

TJ sighed again. She knew there would be no stopping her brother once he'd set his mind to something. 'I swear you're just angling for a free lunch. Sunday it is. But it better be a good story.'

'One that will make your toes curl.'

As she pressed the screen to end the call, TJ pondered on her brother's words. Fingers of apprehension crept up her spine. While the media painted Scott as a rich playboy, her experience of him in the weeks since he'd taken over had shown him in a different light. Would a rich playboy take in a homeless, underage, drug addict? He seemed pretty serious about the business and had taken all the right steps to turn it around. Generally, she was a pretty good judge of character. What exactly had he ended up in court for?

The next morning, her brother's words replayed in her mind as TJ loosened the bolts on Sheila's cylinder head cover and removed it. She eyed it critically, hoping the damage wasn't too severe. Parts were hard to come by, and she didn't have the cash to do modifications.

Outside, she heard the lawnmower and was pleased Tiny was sticking to his word. Over in the rear of the shop, Marty cleaned parts in the machine and whistled tunelessly. This was the longest they'd stayed out of trouble. She hoped it would last. Meanwhile, what Rob had said on the phone rolled around in her head like a loose screw in a toolbox. She'd started to trust Scott Devin, and now Rob had planted seeds of doubt in her mind about him. TJ sighed as she began stripping the cylinder head and placed the parts into a box for Marty to clean next.

'Morning, TJ.'

She stiffened at the sound of Scott's voice. Slowly, she wiped her hands on the rag that lay on top of the radiator before turning to greet him.

'Morning, Scott.'

'How's Sheila doing?'

'We're taking the head off to send to engineering now. Thanks for bringing Tiny in.'

He shrugged. 'No problem since I was coming in any way. Need a hand with that?' He waved a hand toward the engine.

'I thought you had an audit to prepare for?'

'I do. I need a distraction.'

TJ shook her head. 'It's going to get a little crowded under the bonnet when Tiny and Marty get stuck in. But thanks for the offer.'

She ducked her head back into the engine bay and carried on removing parts. When after a couple of minutes more, he still hadn't moved, she asked, 'Something else on your mind?'

'Yes, now that you mention it. My dog arrives tomorrow.'

'That's nice.' Maybe if she ignored him he'd go away.

'What time can I drop him off at your place?'

'Never. He's staying at your mum's place. I don't need a dog.' A cylinder head bolt clanged against nuts and washers as she tossed it into the cardboard box on the floor.

'I think you do.'

'No, I don't. Marty's no trouble.' She wished he would go away. His rich, velvety voice was making her hands sweat.

'But he could be when Tiny moves in.'

Her hands stilled on the spanner. Was he kicking Tiny out already? 'Tiny's staying with you, not me, and even then I don't need a dog.'

'You will when I move in.'

The spanner in TJ's hand slipped, clattered down the side of the engine and out onto the workshop floor.

Cautiously, she straightened and stepped away from Sheila only to back into him where he stood behind her. His hands touched her elbows to steady her. She ignored the shiver his touch sent up her arms and bowed to the flash of anger instead. Pulling away from him, she squatted to retrieve the spanner from under the car.

'I don't remember inviting you to stay.'

'You didn't. But if you have a moment to talk about it, I can explain.'

She straightened to face him. His blue eyes glittered with laughter, and something else she didn't want to explore too deeply — especially considering his eyes had clearly been on her rear as she'd reached under the car.

'The answer will be the same. No.'

'That's because you haven't heard my plan.'

Did he have to be so damned sure of himself? 'I'm not sure I want to hear it.'

He pulled a piece of paper out of his shirt pocket and waved it under her nose. 'You might, if you knew what this is.'

TJ couldn't resist a smile. 'Okay, I'll bite. What is it?'

'I'll tell you over dinner.'

'Don't push your luck. What is it?' She wiped her hands on the rag she pulled from her back pocket.

'This is the council approval for the removal of the

asbestos cladding from your property … and the name of the contractor who'll remove it.'

She took the paper from him and unfolded it carefully. Legal jargon jumped off the white page. She disregarded it as her eyes fell on the approved stamp across the middle of the document. Her heart bumped loudly in her chest and her fingers shook a little.

'How?' she whispered.

'I had a little chat with the mayor last week about the program and how it can work in the council's favour if it was supported by the community. He was impressed by our commitment to extend the program beyond the apprenticeship opportunity.'

'So how come he wasn't impressed when I told him the same thing?'

'It's all in the delivery.'

His smile grew wide with victory, and her heart missed a beat. He really shouldn't smile so often. She was becoming too accustomed to how it lit up his face.

'Dare I ask? No, wait.' She held a hand up as the grin grew wider. 'Maybe it's best that I don't know. There's one small problem.'

'What's that?'

'I can't afford the contractor.' She held the paper out to him, but he didn't take it.

'What if I said that the program funds will cover it?'

'The   grant   doesn't   extend   beyond   the

apprenticeship.' She reached up and tucked the paper back into his pocket.

He caught her hand with his and flattened it against his chest. 'I said funds, not grant. It's in the community's best interests to keep these children off the streets and teach them life skills. As I see it, the building project is an extension of the apprenticeship program. Luckily, the mayor saw it my way, and he's decided to fund a portion of the building costs of your refuge. Which is why he has given you a cheque to cover the removal of the asbestos.'

He lifted her hand away a little to remove another piece of paper from his pocket and unfold it but didn't let go of her hand. He tightened his grip on her fingers as she tugged.

The tugging stilled at the sight of the amount on the cheque. 'That will more than cover the cost of the removal. There'll be small change to buy some new materials.'

'Exactly. This is where you say, "Thank you, Scott".'

'Thank you, Scott.'

He let go of her hand and pocketed the cheque. 'There's one more thing.'

'What?'

'The Police and Citizens Youth Centre will be holding a fundraiser to assist with the cost of the building materials and will help source volunteer tradespeople when the time comes.'

TJ let out a squeal as she launched herself at him, threw her arms around his neck, dragged his head down and planted a kiss squarely on his lips. The moment definitely called for more than a handshake.

'You are a legend! Do you know how hard and long I've fought for this?'

Scott's arms tightened around her as he hugged her closer. 'No, but if I'd known this would be the reaction, I might have intervened a whole lot sooner.'

TJ laughed and kissed him again, on the cheek this time. 'Thank you, Scott. I really can't say that enough.' She wriggled in his arms. 'I need to tell the boys.'

'In a minute,' he said as his arms tightened and he lowered his head.

Chapter Eight

‘So, this is what you call working?’

TJ tore out of Scott's arms at the sound of her brother's voice. He released her reluctantly. Damn it, he hadn't even touched her lips yet.

He watched with regret as TJ launched herself at Rob and hugged him tightly.

‘Guess what?’

‘What?’ Rob replied as he kissed her forehead. Over her head, Rob's eyes narrowed on Scott.

‘We've got funding!’

‘No shit? From where?’

‘Scott had a little chat to the mayor.’

‘You mean Mr Bloody *Professional Spotlight* Devin?’

TJ punched his arm. He let her go and walked over to shake Scott's hand.

'Rob. Nice to see you again.' Scott accepted the handshake.

For a moment they squared up as Rob studied his face.

'What exactly are you up to with my sister?'

Scott laughed. 'At ease, soldier. You have nothing to worry about. TJ was thanking me for her cheque from the mayor.'

'Right.' Rob drawled the word. 'Don't make me get the shotgun out.'

TJ rolled her eyes. 'Like you'd even know how to use one. Mind your own business.'

Rob grinned and turned his attention back to Scott. 'So, tell me how you squeezed funds out of the mayor.'

'Like I told TJ, it's all in the delivery.' Scott shrugged.

'Not like you were delivering to my sister there when I walked in, I hope?'

Scott laughed. 'No. Nothing like that at all. Your sister was expressing her gratitude.'

'Yes, I could see she was very grateful.' He turned to TJ. 'You'll have to tell me more. I wanted to pop in and say hi to Sheila, really. I have a present for her.'

'Really? You mean you opened your wallet and let the moths out?' TJ mocked.

'Accountants aren't tight arses, Titch, we're just careful with money.' Rob smiled as he pulled a small box out from behind his back. 'A new radiator cap.'

TJ laughed. 'I'm sure she'll be happy with it! Thanks, Rob.'

'It's good to see you laughing again. I know how hard these last few months have been.' He turned back to Scott. 'Thanks for putting that smile back on her face. I'm pleased she finally has the backup she needs.'

'TJ has a good thing going with the program. It's making a difference to young lives. Why don't we all grab a cup of coffee in my office to celebrate?'

'You guys go on. I'll be there in a minute. I'll sort Marty out with what he needs to do first.'

TJ was stalling and Scott knew it. The colour in her cheeks was high as her eyes refused to meet his. He'd give her a moment to recoup. God knows, he needed one himself. He hadn't expected her to feel like she belonged in his arms.

'Sure. I'll get your coffee ready.' Scott led Rob away.

'You must have some swing with the mayor then?' Rob followed behind, matching Scott's strides.

Scott shrugged as he opened the door to his office and stepped aside for Rob to go inside. 'I figured TJ needed a little help. The program should have the support of the community.'

'We've been trying to achieve that for so long. I thought TJ would give it up, but those kids mean a lot to her.' Rob stopped and looked around the room. 'She fought long and hard with Mal Malone to get it all going. All he saw was the dollar signs that the grant would bring in. He never gave any thought to the kids in the program.' He turned back to where Scott lined up the coffee cups. 'TJ was pretty much left to run the whole thing. It was just as well she had Ethan Wright to give her support.'

'Yeah, he seems pretty committed too. Nice bloke. I've been doing some work with him to find out more about other rehabilitation programs available.' Scott placed a cup under the spout of the coffee machine.

'So, what were you doing trying to kiss my sister?'

Rob's words threw him off guard a little, even though he'd been expecting them. Scott cleared his throat. What could he say to the brother of the girl he'd been caught with his hands all over? A girl who'd crept under his skin and into his heart because of her spirit and selfless determination. One who'd begun to restore his faith in humanity and melt the ice that had held him in its grip since the court case. He took a moment to answer as he ran his hand across his jaw.

'She's quite a girl.'

'Yes she is, but that doesn't answer my question.'

'I know. It was exactly as you saw it. I won't deny that I am attracted to her.'

'Like you were attracted to Serena Snow?'

Scott dropped his hand to his side as he turned to the coffee machine. 'No. Nothing like Serena Snow.'

And, he realised, he was right. What he'd seen in Serena was nothing compared to what he saw in TJ. They were poles apart. One held the world in her hands and the other had the world at her feet. Serena revelled in stomping on the world and TJ was all about picking it up again.

'That was messy business, Scott. I don't want it transferred to my sister. She has enough to deal with.'

'Point taken,' he replied as the door opened and TJ came into the room. He handed her the coffee he'd just poured. 'Everything okay?'

TJ carefully avoided contact as she took the cup. 'Yes. Tiny's done with mowing the verge. He's helping Marty on Sheila now … unless you want him to do something else.' Her gaze flew to his, full of questions and uncertainty, as stirred up as he was over that encounter.

Maybe one kiss would be enough to satisfy their curiosity. 'No, let them play a bit. Shall we sit down, and I'll tell you my plan?' He pulled another chair closer for Rob. 'Once the asbestos is removed, building can go ahead. I promised the mayor that Mal's Motors would pitch in with volunteer help from the staff to show community support for the program.'

'That might encourage some of the locals to participate too,' Rob countered.

'Exactly. The mayor has also said he will encourage

some of the local tradespeople to pitch in with things like plumbing, roofing, carpentry and so on.'

'Wow, that must have been some pitch you delivered. Either he's had a change of heart, or you've been able to make him see something we couldn't.'

Scott laughed. 'I've mastered the art of negotiation, and a promise of a donation to the local arts centre helped to sweeten the deal. But there's more.'

TJ sat up in her chair. 'There's always more. I'm guessing he has some reservations about the impact of juvenile delinquents in the community. That was one of the concerns when we approached him.'

'Yes, he is concerned. Which is why I have a suggestion to make.' He paused to pick up a pen from his desk and tapped it on his palm. 'He's asked for round-the-clock supervision of the boys for as long as they are on your property during the building process.'

TJ sighed. 'I can understand that. I'm perfectly capable of looking after the boys. Bill and Rose come over all the time when they're there, and Ethan stops in twice a week, as does Rob.'

'That's not enough for the mayor. He's worried about you alone with a group of teenagers who have yet to prove that they're on the straight and narrow.' He reached out to cover her hand with his as TJ looked like she was about to argue. 'Hear me out first. It's not that he doesn't trust you. He really is worried about your wellbeing. It's tough raising teenagers. More so when you're not their parent.'

TJ pulled her hand out from under his and clasped hers in her lap. 'So, what's the plan?'

'I think that Tiny and Marty would be a lot happier if they were together. Tiny's doing okay with me so far, but I can see the boredom setting in. He needs to have company his own age. I can't stop him going out on his own if he decides to, but I would like to discourage it.'

'You want them both to stay with TJ?' Concern etched Rob's face. 'Tiny clearly has a problem with her. When you're around, he'll toe the line, but when you're not …?'

'Which is why I have a proposal to make. I need to look for another place to stay. The townhouse was always meant to be a temporary arrangement. I'm not ready to buy a property yet. I'm a little over inner city living, but I'm not sure that I'm ready for semi-rural either.' He turned to TJ. 'So, I figured if I could rent two rooms from you while we're working on the rebuilding of the cabins, I'll have a place to keep my dog and get a feel for whether I can do the semi-rural thing or not. Tiny will have Marty for company and together we can make sure that they both stay out of trouble.'

'Why can't you stay with your parents? They live next door.' TJ sat on the edge of her seat, clearly uncomfortable and not convinced.

'Because Tiny won't give you any trouble if I'm

there. Sarge, my dog, will be an added bonus, both as a distraction and as extra security. Research has proved that dogs — and pets in general — have a positive impact on negative behaviour in children. It's worth a try. Plus, you'll have a steady income from the room rentals to subsidise any improvements to the property. I'll pay you for room and board for both Tiny and myself. Plus, I'll be there to help with the supervision of the building works.'

Scott sat back and folded his arms, allowing the thought to lie between them. TJ looked at Rob, who shrugged.

'It sounds like a good plan. TJ?'

TJ stood up and wandered over to the window. She placed her hands on the sill and stared out over the hills. Scott watched her consider his proposal. He could almost hear the wheels turning as she chewed her bottom lip. He'd promised the mayor he would keep a close eye on the boys. Having them all under the same roof seemed like the best solution. Sarge would love the company, and he could do with the change of scenery.

'Why?'

'Why what?' Scott stood up to stand beside her.

'Why are you doing this? We've managed perfectly fine without you until now.'

'Because I've been looking for something, and this feels like the right thing to do. I came back here looking for a project, a new challenge. Buying another struggling dealership wasn't enough this time. It hasn't fulfilled that need I've been trying to satisfy. Dealing with these kids has given me that sense of satisfaction, that challenge I've been looking for.'

'I don't suppose it had anything to do with running away from Serena Snow, then.' TJ turned and looked him in the eye, set a challenge.

He considered the challenge and met it as he stared back. 'No. I don't back down from a fight, TJ,' he said without as much as a blink. 'I stay and fight. Serena lost, I won. Let's get that skeleton out of the closet right now.' He turned to Rob. 'And then I can put your mind at rest too. Anyone for more coffee?'

TJ shook her head and sat on the edge of his desk. He could feel her eyes on his back as he poured the coffee. Serena's skeleton was one he'd gladly lay to rest and hoped it would stay there once he had. Yes, he'd crossed the country to get away from her. There was no denying that. The peace and quiet of the west coast had beckoned, with the added bonus of his parents being a little closer. The business opportunity had been more of an experiment than an investment. He'd played with much higher stakes on the east coast. Mal's Motors was child's play in comparison.

'Serena and I had a brief relationship. She was my employee, a very ambitious one. Unfortunately, she used her power as my girlfriend to bully the staff, and it backfired. We got taken to court for harassment. The employee won and the charge was against Serena but, as the business owner, it was my duty of care to prevent it. Serena was too ambitious to take the fall alone, so she counter sued me for harassment, stating that I'd coerced her into a relationship.'

'And did you?'

His laugh was tinged with bitterness as he sat down again. He picked up his mobile phone off the desk and wiggled it in the air. 'These things have a habit of dropping you right in it. What she didn't tell the judge was that she initiated the chats. All her messages in response were deleted from her phone. There's a whole lot more to the story, and I won't bore you with the details, but the judge threw it out of court because of insufficient evidence. What I will tell you is that no coercing was required.'

'But the media had a field day with the story,' Rob countered.

'Yes, they did. Unfortunately, some of the mud sticks, which is why I decided to make the move out here. In the hope that the media would find something else to focus on.'

'Does this mean your involvement in the program is only to garner positive media and get you back into their good books?' Silence sliced the tension in the room as TJ's words fell like splintering glass between them.

Scott's eyes narrowed on hers as he bit down on his anger. He stood slowly and came around the desk to face her. 'Back off, Tiger. I don't like what you're suggesting.'

She hopped off the desk to face him, drew herself up to her full height and held his angry stare. 'And I don't like you using the program as a springboard to rescue your reputation.'

'That's not what I'm doing, and deep down, you know it. I please myself and I pick my fights. I don't want to argue with you, TJ, but I do want to join your fight for these kids.'

Rob stepped into the fray. He placed his hand on TJ's arm. 'Sit down, TJ. It won't kill you to listen to what Scott has in mind. It won't hurt to accept help either. You've fought this alone for too long. I can't be there as much as I would like to. I'd be happier with Scott staying with you and the boys.'

'I've been coping just fine on my own.' Emotions chased across TJ's face, alternating between stubbornness and uncertainty.

Scott sighed as studied her. He admired her determination and commitment — yet another way in which she differed so much from Serena. Ambition didn't come into it at all. 'I'm picking my dog up from the airport tomorrow. I'll bring him around to your place. We can discuss it with Marty and Tiny and see what they think.'

Rob agreed. 'Great idea, Scott. I'll be there too, so we can go over the finer details. I have to go, guys. I've got a meeting with a client. TJ, please hear Scott out before you veto the idea completely.'

TJ nodded, but her eyes were on Scott's, as if she were trying to read the thoughts in his head. That was what he liked most about her. What you saw was what you got. Every emotion, every thought, every action was right there on the surface. He had no doubt she would tackle anything thrown her way.

Rob bent to kiss her cheek before extending his hand to shake Scott's. 'I'll see you tomorrow.'

'Yes. We have some planning to do, if TJ agrees.' Scott walked to the door with Rob.

'Give her time. She likes to process. She'll see sense eventually.'

'I'm still in the room, Robert!'

'And she only calls me Robert when I'm in trouble.' He blew her a kiss as Scott closed the door behind him.

'Do you want to think about this overnight? I'm worried about you, TJ.' Scott moved back to where TJ stood. 'I read the reports from juvie hall. The psychologist who treated Tiny is convinced that his dangerous behaviour will escalate. I'd like to prove him wrong, and I do believe we can help him if we get this project off the ground.'

'What you're saying makes sense. I appreciate your commitment to the program. It's what's between us that I have a problem with.' TJ paced the floor. 'We can't afford to cross that invisible line between being colleagues and being more than that, Scott. If Rob hadn't arrived when he did …'

He raked a hand through his hair as he perched on the edge of his desk. 'If you don't want it to happen again, it won't.'

'And if I had a dollar for every time I'd heard that line, I wouldn't need funding for the building project.'

He smiled and put out a hand to stop her pacing. His fingers slid down her arm to link with hers. A gentle tug brought her closer. Her free hand pressed against his chest to stop him.

'I'm a man of my word, TJ. The next move, if there is one, will be yours.' He dropped her hands and stood before pulling the paperwork and cheque out of his pocket once more. 'Take these and think over them tonight. We'll talk about it again in the morning. Once you're happy to proceed, we can get the ball rolling. The contractor has been notified that we will contact him within the next few days to start clearing the asbestos cladding. The sooner we get this happening, the happier everyone will be. Now, I'd better get some work done. It might be an idea to go and see what the boys are up to.'

'Thank you, Scott, but we do need to set ground rules.'

'I know.'

Rules, lines that couldn't be crossed, temptation that would always be one step away, and the unavoidable office gossip that would result when the news got around that he was boarding with her. It could all go horribly wrong very quickly. As he watched her walk out of his office, he knew that he would do whatever he could to make TJ's project a success. What he wasn't ready to do was ask himself why. The answer would be too close to be admitting he cared.

Chapter Nine

Sunday dawned sunny and bright. TJ hoped that was a good omen as she knocked on Marty's bedroom door. 'Come on, big guy, it's almost time for breakfast.'

A muffled groan came from inside, followed by a thump and a muttered oath. 'Is it 6am already? Fuck, TJ, why do we have to get up so early? It's Sunday.' The door opened and he poked his head out.

TJ grinned. 'Watch your language.' She tugged his sleep-spiked hair gently. 'We've got chores to do. You need to collect the chook eggs, and I'm going to get the pork roast on the go for lunch.'

'It's bloody sparrow's fart! Can't the eggs wait?'

'Not if you want breakfast. Smell that?' She sniffed the air. 'That's fresh bread. You don't get any until you've collected the eggs.'

Marty sniffed the air too. 'Fu—' He stopped at TJ's warning look. 'Far out. It does smell good.'

They laughed as Marty's stomach growled in response.

'Off you go. To the shower and then hit the chook pen. Or maybe chook pen then shower.' She wrinkled her nose as she walked passed him toward the kitchen.

'Hey, TJ?' He waited for her to turn around. 'Thanks.'

TJ smiled. A simple word held so much weight. 'You don't need to thank me. I have some good news to share when the others get here. Things are looking up.'

'They are? Like how?'

'You'll have to wait until the others arrive. I only want to tell it once. Come on, let's get breakfast out of the way first. Hurry now.'

They did the chores in easy harmony. It was at times like these that TJ's heart glowed with hope. And pride. These were the times when she saw the potential in Marty. He enjoyed pottering around on the property, fixing fences, cutting firebreaks and mucking out the chook pen. The dark world of drugs and troubled teenagers seemed so far away as the sun warmed the blue sky.

If only she could help Tiny find the same inner peace that Marty found out here. She'd spent a sleepless night tossing over Scott's proposal. Everything made sense, except the bit about having him in her house every day and every night.

Despite the inner alarm bells over the case with Serena Snow, the attraction between them was strong. Scott was strong. And she'd been fighting alone for so long now. It would be nice to have someone else shoulder some of the responsibilities. Not that Rob didn't try. He did his best, but he couldn't see the same value in the project that she did. That Scott did see the value warmed her heart a little more toward him each day. And it was with each warming that came the danger of falling in love with him. TJ straightened from putting the roast in the oven. *Oh, God.* She was falling in love with him.

'Shit!'

'Wassup, TJ? You okay?' Marty stepped into the kitchen just as the sound of a car coming up the drive reached them. 'Mr D and Tiny are here.'

With a hand that shook just a little, TJ took her apron off and hung it on the pantry door. 'All good, Marty. Let's go say hi.'

They stepped out onto the veranda as Scott's ute came to a stop on the gravel drive. In the back was a massive black and brown beast with a head the size of a beer barrel.

'Fu … Phwoar, TJ! Is that a dog or a horse?' Marty hissed in her ear.

She nudged him with her shoulder. 'Don't let Scott

hear you say that, but to answer your question, I think it's a beast.'

They watched as Scott and Tiny got out of the ute. Tiny bounded up the stairs to envelop Marty in their ritualistic man-hug — a quick bump of the shoulders, a clasp of right hands, a pat on the back and a knuckle bump. Tiny touched the peak of his cap.

'Hey, TJ.'

'Hi, Tiny. What the hell is that thing?'

Tiny laughed and TJ's heart swelled. Tiny never laughed, not even at jokes, and especially never at anything she said. Perhaps they really had turned a corner.

'That's Sarge, Mr D's Rottweiler. Picked him up from the airport this morning. Pretty cool, huh?'

'I'm not sure cool is a word I'd use …' Her eyes were glued to the dog as Scott unclipped his harness and set him free. With a single command, the dog jumped out of the ute and sat at Scott's feet. Another command and the dog went to heel.

'Is he showing off?' She nudged Marty again.

Marty grinned. 'I think he's trying to impress you, TJ.'

'Ha! I'm not impressed. I'm paralysed. Good God, how much would that beast eat? I hope he's vegetarian. He looks like he could swallow you whole.'

'Mr D says he'll only do that on command.'

She was sure Tiny was only half joking. Muscles

rippled in unison as Scott and the dog walked toward the veranda. TJ was hard pressed to keep her eyes on the dog any longer as they came closer. 'Tiny, were you guys at footy training this morning?'

'Yeah. There was a friendlies game at the oval near Mr D's place this morning, so we went down to check it out. Then we had to go pick up the beast, so we didn't have time to change.'

Her mind vaguely registered that Tiny had just spoken the longest sentence she'd ever heard from him. Her focus had been on the six feet-plus of muscle that strolled toward her dressed in tight football shorts. Once white, they were now streaked with mud and grass stains. The red and white sleeveless guernsey clung to a strong, wide chest and shoulders, showcasing arms sculptured with muscle. *Oh, dear lord.* She was in trouble.

'Towels.' The word came out on a whisper.

'What's that, TJ?'

'Towels, Marty. Get them towels. Shower. Tiny, you go first.' She turned to Tiny and realised his face was streaked with mud and sweat ... and his grin was wider than she'd ever seen before. She grinned back, and the boys took off at a sprint, their voices booming through the house.

'Morning, TJ.' Scott stopped at the stairs to the veranda and commanded the dog to sit. 'Say hi to Sarge.'

She eyed the dog warily. 'Has he eaten?'

Scott laughed. 'Yes. A football team.'

'Ah, well. That's okay then. Hi, Sarge.'

Sarge barked and held up a paw. TJ felt her heart melt as he cocked his head and frowned. She stepped down and shook his paw. Scott slipped him a treat.

'Enjoy your game?' she asked, keeping her gaze firmly on the dog.

'Yes, actually. Tiny is quite a good player. I think he enjoyed himself.'

TJ scratched behind Sarge's ear and smiled at the dopey look in his eyes. 'That's good. It's the first time I've seen him smile.'

'Really?'

'Yes.' She forced her eyes past his impressive body and met his eyes. 'Thank you.'

'Thank me later.' His eyes glittered and his lips twitched.

She found herself smiling back. 'In your dreams. I have beer. Cold beer. That should be thanks enough.'

He threw a friendly arm around her shoulders and steered her toward the house. 'I accept that offer. For now.'

'Ha! I think a shower is in order first. Since Tiny is using the second bathroom, you can use mine. Go easy on my Chanel.'

The arm around her shoulders crept up around her neck and pulled her closer. He buried his face against her hair for a moment before kissing her temple. 'Bless you, Tiger. You smell like fresh bread and Sunday roast. Makes a change from grease and oil.'

She elbowed him in the stomach, impressed when it met washboard abs that didn't give way to fleshiness. 'Yes, well I think Sarge smells better than you do right now. Go on. To the shower. Will he stay with me?' She shrugged off his arm, walked up the stairs and through the front door as dog and man followed closely.

'Yes. Stay, Sarge. Which way to your bedroom?'

TJ swallowed. Those dark velvet tones made it sound like an invitation. 'Down the hall and to the left. On your way past, ask Marty for a towel and shower gel. Unless you want to smell like roses.'

He spun her around and took her face in his hands. 'Slap me if you want to.'

She had a nanosecond to see the challenge in his eyes before he kissed her hard. Firm, warm lips teased hers, angled to deepen the kiss. Time melted away as TJ stilled under his hands and he coaxed her lips with his.

It took all her strength not to return the kiss. He even tasted like dark velvet. Like sin. Like something she shouldn't be tasting. She pulled away, placed her hands over his and removed them from her face. The glint in his eyes shouted victory as hers slid away to look over his shoulder.

'Rules. Boundaries. Shower,' she reminded him.

He stepped back and peeled the sweaty guernsey

over his head to reveal a sun-kissed chest sprinkled with a light dusting of dark hair, and a cheeky smile.

'You taste like temptation, TJ.' He stepped around her and walked inside.

This was so not going to work. A bad, *bad* idea. She watched as he disappeared up the hallway, her hands cupping hot cheeks. Those shorts showcased a very nice arse. One she was about to see around her house every day if she agreed to his plan. Oh boy, was she in trouble ...

'Yoo-hoo!' Rose's voice rang out, thankfully redirecting her thoughts and her attention. She kissed Rose's cheek affectionately, accepted Bill's hug and returned it.

'I see Scott's here already.' Bill released her to look up the hallway. 'Did he pick up his dog?'

'The boys are cleaning up after playing a game of footy this morning. They'll be out soon. Sarge is standing guard over the pork roast in the oven. I think he's hoping there's a bone in there for him. What's for dessert?'

Rose held up the basket in her hand. 'Apple and rhubarb pie with custard and cream.'

'Ooh, yum!' TJ lifted the blue chequered cloth that covered the contents of the basket. 'Still warm. Let's put it in the kitchen, and I'll make us a cup of tea. Bill, the telly's on in the lounge if you want to wait in there for the boys.'

'Will do, love, thanks.' He wandered off, happy to be relieved of kitchen duties.

'Need help with anything,' Rose asked as they entered the homely, country-style kitchen.

TJ loved her kitchen. The forest green walls blended beautifully with the rich, bare Oregon pine ceilings, the walls lined with the same cabinetry her grandfather had hand-crafted when he'd built the house in the 1940s. Their leadlight, bevelled-glass fronts showcased her grandmother's collection of antique chinaware. Here she always felt at home, at peace.

'Do you want to peel the potatoes for roasting while I prep the rest of the veggies?' She put the basket on the table in the centre of the kitchen and waved toward the pile of vegetables resting on the stone bench tops.

'Sure! Then you can tell me all the latest gossip. How are the boys doing?'

'They seem to be doing fine. Tiny seems very happy staying with Scott. He actually smiled today and completed a sentence without grunting once.'

Rose laughed. 'That's progress. But you know, love, grunting is all part of teenage-speak. Nothing's changed since Scott was one. Must be a boy thing, hey? What about Marty?'

TJ made their tea as Rose moved to the kitchen sink to peel the potatoes.

'He's doing okay. I had to go and pick up his things from his mum's. She sent me a text to say they'd be out on the lawn for him, and if I didn't pick them up, the council would when they do the verge collections.'

'Oh, that's sad. The poor kid. He must have taken that hard.'

'I had a chat to him about it. She has problems of her own, too, and he understands that. But it still hurts. Other than that, he's happy. We get along fine together, and he's a good kid. As long as I can keep both of them off the drugs, they'll be fine. This is the longest they've behaved.' She carried the steaming mugs of fragrant peppermint tea across to the kitchen bench and handed one to Rose.

'Thanks, love. I'm glad Scott has taken an interest in the program. How are you two getting along?'

TJ's hand paused on a bunch of spinach as she searched for something neutral to say. 'He's a very generous boss.'

Rose laughed and hugged her tightly. 'Oh, TJ, you know that's not what I meant. How are you getting along on a personal level?'

'He's my boss, and that's the way it will stay. I can't afford for it to be more, Rose,' she replied gently, turning on the tap to rinse the greens. 'Please, no matchmaking.'

'Life has a way of choosing for us. You two don't need my help. I can see it when you're together. You're perfect for each other.'

'Workplace relationships always end badly. I can't afford to lose my job.'

'Oh, poppycock.' Rose patted her hand. 'Couples run businesses together successfully every day. If the relationship is built on a solid foundation, the small things won't matter.'

'It won't work, Rose. We're too different.'

She shook the water from the spinach and placed it in the colander. Deep voices from the hallway saved her from having to continue the conversation. She loved Rose and Bill like the parents she'd never known. As much as she appreciated that Rose only wanted to see her happy, she could never find that happiness with their son.

Sarge rose from standing guard over the oven, barked once and ambled over as the men spilled noisily into the kitchen. The fridge door thumped, cold drinks were handed around and stubby holders tossed through the air as they re-enacted football passes. Chairs scraped around the kitchen table as they sat and swapped football scores. Scott retrieved the basket from the middle of the table and carried it over to the kitchen bench. He threw an arm around each of their shoulders before kissing his mum's cheek.

'Hi, Mum.'

'Hello, love. I heard you've been playing footy. Did you have fun?'

'Didn't realise how much I'd missed it.' He bent his head to kiss TJ's cheek.

She backed away with a warning look. 'Rule number one: my space …' she warned with a flip of the tea towel between them and a finger to his chest to press him back a step. '… Your space.'

He grimaced and patted her head instead, pretending he didn't see the narrowing of her eyes on his.

Rose smiled at them both indulgently before raising a perfectly groomed eyebrow at TJ. *See?*

TJ ignored her look and began peeling carrots as Scott wandered away to join in the debate about who would win the premiership.

The front door slammed, and heavy footfalls echoed in the hallway. Sarge sat to attention and growled low.

'Friend, Sarge.' Scott ruffled the dog's ears as Rob stuck his head around the door of the kitchen. 'Hey, Rob.'

'Hey,' said Rob amidst a flurry of greetings. 'Holy shit! What is that beast?'

'This is Sarge. He's accepted the position of home security and is waiting on approval from the boss to start.' Scott nodded in TJ's direction.

'Jeez, he's huge. Will we need to arrange a second mortgage to feed him?'

'Nah, the occasional burglar or intruder will satisfy him.'

'Why do I get the feeling you're only half joking?

Hey there, little sister.' Rob hugged TJ and kissed Rose's cheek. 'Rose, I smell your rhubarb pie. God bless you. What time is lunch so we can get to dessert?'

Rose smiled and waved him away. 'You have to eat all your veggies first, Robert.'

'Ahh, Rose, but I'm a meat man.'

'No veggies, no dessert!' Rose waved a finger at him playfully.

'You drive a hard bargain.' He wandered over to the table and accepted the beer Scott held out to him. 'So, what's been happening here?'

As the noise level rose and their voices boomed around the house, TJ couldn't help but feel that her grandfather was smiling down on them right now. He'd loved having a household full of people on a Sunday. The house seemed alive again as hope shimmered on the horizon for the building project. She hoped they could keep it that way for as long as they could.

Lunch was a boisterous affair in the dining room of the cottage, and Scott realized it had been a very long time since he'd enjoyed one quite so much. Tiny and Marty had come alive, faces beaming as they were embraced into the family and encouraged to join in on conversations. He was proud to have a father who showed interest in these lost boys. His encouragement had them chatting and laughing happily — even Tiny who, until today, had barely strung a sentence together.

It seemed he was making up for his silence now as he shared an amazing knowledge of football history. He studied the animation on the boy's face as he related a story. Here was the passion that needed to be embraced, the energy that needed to be harnessed. He made a mental note to sign him up for the local football team when they moved in with TJ.

TJ … Dressed in those damn denim cut-offs again that showed off firm, long, brown legs so well. Her fuchsia pink t-shirt clung lovingly to her chest and declared *my eyes are up here* with an arrow pointing up. He watched as she chatted easily with his mother. The taste of her lips still lingered on his. A damn silly thing to do. Why had he given in to the impulse? Now he wanted more. Way more, he realised, than he'd ever wanted from Serena. With Serena, it had been a mutual arrangement. One he'd known had no future even before he'd realised what she was up to. He'd never yearned for her company like he did for TJ's.

She caught him looking. 'What?'

'Nothing. More wine?'

She frowned at him and pushed her empty plate aside.

'Thanks.' She held out her glass for him to top up. 'Something on your mind?'

'It'll keep. Should we talk about the project before we have dessert?'

'I guess,' she replied, putting her glass down to stand and collect the plates.

He stood and helped her clear away, refusing the offers of help from around the table. 'Relax. We've got it.'

He followed her into the kitchen where they cleared the plates in silence. He made a couple of trips to retrieve dishes while she rinsed and packed them in the dishwasher.

'The boys seem relaxed and happy,' he said as he came back with the last load of dishes.

'Yes, they do. I'm so glad. At last, I can see a future for them. Thank you, Scott. I'll never be able to say that enough.' She closed the door of the dishwasher and set it to run.

'I'm glad I could help. We need to talk about the rest of the plan. Like when Tiny and I can move in so we can get started. I think it's important we don't delay it. We need to keep the momentum going so that the boys stay interested and motivated.'

TJ placed the dessert in the oven and set the dial to warm before answering. 'I agree. My concern is what the gossips will say when they find out. Your plan makes perfect sense, and I sure could use the rent money, but the effect it could have if it all went wrong between us is what worries me.'

'I won't tolerate gossip.'

'You won't be able to stop it.' Office gossip tended to have a life of its own at Mal's Motors.

'We'll deal with it when it happens. I won't let anything hurt you or the boys, TJ. You have to believe that.'

'It's not always in your control. Especially not with your past. The gossip mill is already running hot as to who you'll hook up with next. There are a few girls who would happily put their hand up, too, I'm sure.'

'Damn, it's hard living up to my media image …' His eyes teased hers as she smiled mockingly at him. 'That's why I need you — to protect me from the hordes of socialites and groupies hammering at my door.'

'You flatter yourself. It's Sarge they're really after.'

'You see? That's why I love you. You're a balm for my ego.'

Ignoring the rollercoaster ride her stomach took at that, she opened the fridge and removed the raw pork bone cut from the roast earlier. 'Come, Sarge. This will keep your hunger at bay until we find you a baddie to eat.' She waved the bone under his nose and led him to the back door. 'Sit. Paw.' He shook, took the bone from her hand and lay outside on the back veranda. 'Come back in when you're done but leave the bone outside, okay?'

Big brown eyes stared deliriously at her as Sarge drooled over his bone waiting for the command to eat.

'Go!' She stepped back inside and straight into Scott's arms.

'That's another reason I like you. You're kind to my dog.'

'That's not a dog, that's a 60kg man-eating beast. Of course I'm going to be kind. Hands off, please.'

He tightened his arms around her instead. 'Can't. For some reason, you drive me crazy. You've been driving me crazy all week. I smell your goddamn perfume everywhere. I hear your voice every time you raise it. I see you walking in those damned stilettos and miniskirts. And worst of all, since when are steel-capped boots and overalls so damned sexy?'

She placed her hands on his forearms and pushed. 'This is what I mean. We can't share a house if you're going to keep this up. We need rules. Lines need to be drawn. This cannot happen between us. Scott —'

He swallowed the words from her parted lips as he pulled her closer to him, caressing her back with splayed fingers as the feel of her body against his robbed him of coherent thought.

TJ struggled to remember the rules herself as she placed her hand on his chest, intent on pushing him away. She lost the willpower as her hand came to rest against his warmth. He nibbled her lip. Heat blazed between them as her hand moved to caress the hot skin of his cheek. He slid his hand down her back to cup her bottom and pull her closer still. A purr rose in her throat at the contact.

Vaguely, she heard common sense telling her to stop. She ignored it as his lips moved to her throat, tipping her head back. Her breasts rubbed against his chest as he followed the trail to nibble her ear lobe. When she moaned, he took her lips again to silence her. Somewhere, somehow in the madness, they'd moved. He leaned back against the kitchen bench, legs spread with her between them.

'TJ? Scott? What's taking you guys so long? We're hanging out for dessert here!' Rob's voice rang out from the dining room.

Scott dragged his lips from hers and held her close for a moment as their heartbeats pounded against each other. She slipped out of his arms and crossed the room, refusing to look at him.

'I think we just crossed the line. That got out of hand. I'm sorry.'

TJ held up her hand. 'Whatever you do, don't spoil it by apologising. Let's not dissect this right now.' Her hand shook as she moved to take the dessert bowls out of the cupboard. Wordlessly, she walked back to where he stood to set them out on the bench top as Rose appeared in the kitchen doorway.

'Everything okay in here?' Her gaze swung between them as tension hung in the air like a tightly coiled spring. 'Scott? TJ?'

'I'm going to take a walk. Save me some pie.' Scott sauntered through the back door, whistling for Sarge as he went. Sarge eyed him for a moment and went back to chewing his bone. 'Damn traitor,' Scott muttered and walked away.

Rose walked over to where TJ stood 'Everything okay, sweetheart? Did you two have an argument?'

TJ busied herself with gathering spoons for the dessert, unable to meet Scott's mother's eyes, her colour high. 'It's fine. A small misunderstanding, that's all.'

Rose's eyes wandered over her swollen lips, her ruffled hair and her T-shirt, scrunched at the sides. 'I'll give you a moment to gather yourself.' She piled up the dessert bowls and placed the spoons into the one on top. 'Bring the rhubarb pie through when you're ready.' Rose strode out, trying hard not to smile.

Chapter Ten

The afternoon passed uneventfully, with TJ avoiding Scott as much as possible. Everything about his plan looked like it was going to go south, fast. There was no way they could live in the same house with this attraction simmering between them. Not even for the boys.

On the other hand, she really needed the income the rent would bring. It would help strengthen her position with the bank — perhaps even keep foreclosure at bay a little longer. And watching how Marty and Tiny had come to life today, she knew she didn't have it in her heart to deny them the chance for a better life.

She'd just have to find a way to deal with Scott until he lost interest and moved on. That's what guys like him did. He'd lose interest in her once he realised she was more the stay-at-home kind than the party animals he was used to. She dressed up once a year for the industry awards and that was it. She only owned one party dress. Yes, she'd have to make sure he lost interest quickly.

The boys were happy, and that's what counted. Rose and Bill had wandered off home after lunch, leaving Rob, Scott and the boys to kick the football around in the clearing by the creek. Their laughter and shouts paid testimony to their happiness. Sarge lay snoring happily at her feet as she sat in her deck chair on the veranda and watched. Her initial concerns about having the dog had been dispelled. He was friendly but watchful. And both boys seemed to have taken a liking to him, which was a good thing.

Normally she would have joined in the football game, but for now she needed to get her head around having three males and a dog invading her space on a more permanent basis. Her peaceful nights would be sacrificed for boisterous conversations and fighting over the television remote. Would it be too much? Living *and* working with them? Time would tell.

She saw Scott making his way up from the creek and went inside to get him a bottle of water from the fridge. When she came back out, he was sitting in her chair, scratching the dog's ears.

'Good game?'

'Yeah. The boys won.'

She held out the bottle of water. 'Thought you might need this.'

'Cheers.' He took the bottle, twisted off the cap and drank deeply.

She watched as his throat worked and his eyes avoided hers. Silence stretched between them awkwardly. TJ sighed. 'Scott, we need to talk about what happened earlier.'

'I'm not going to apologise.'

'No, I don't need an apology. If you and Tiny are going to move in, it can't happen again.'

'I thought you might change your mind about us moving in.'

'No, I can't do that to the boys. For their sakes, I have to get this project off the ground.'

She sat down on the wooden decking next to the dog. Sarge abandoned his ear scratch to cuddle closer to her side and lay his big head in her lap. Sleepy brown eyes gazed into hers as she stroked the wrinkled forehead.

'It won't happen again, but I'm not going to deny that I have feelings for you, TJ. I like you. You're easy to talk to. No bullshit, only plain speaking. It's a refreshing change.' Scott leaned back in the deck chair and closed his eyes.

'Thank you … I think. So, when did you want to move in?'

He raised a hand and rubbed his eyes wearily. 'I haven't got much to move, so how about tomorrow after work I start bringing things over? I need to give notice on the townhouse. The landlord's pretty flexible with rentals in such short supply.'

'I'll get the rooms ready then. Have you told Tiny yet?'

'No, I thought it best if we tell them together. It's still your project.' He turned his head to look at her. 'Want to tell them now?'

Her heart bumped as she met his piercing blue gaze. She took the leap, knowing her life was about to change. For better or worse? She was about to find out.

'Yes, let's take a walk down there.'

He stood and extended a hand to help her up. With only the slightest of hesitation, she placed her hand in his. He tugged her up and they stood inches apart. For a moment she thought he would kiss her again. Instead, he let go of her hand and stepped back.

'Let's go, Sarge.' He whistled, and the dog stood up next to him. 'Are you coming?' He looked back at TJ.

She nodded, wondering why she felt so bereft. 'You go on. I'll catch up. The boys will be thirsty, so I'll bring some water for them.'

'So, we're good then?' Scott didn't turn around as he asked the question. Instead, he looked across the valley as the sun started to sink toward the treetops.

'We're good.'

He nodded and set off down to the creek with Sarge loping at his side.

There was no getting away from the fact that the

coming weeks were going to be difficult as they all adjusted to living and working together. TJ walked into the kitchen and retrieved three water bottles from the fridge. The hardest adjustment would be knowing there was a complicated, incredibly sexy man in the room next door to hers who was completely out of bounds. They might have stood a chance at a relationship if they didn't work together. Even then, they were chalk and cheese. Worlds apart. As condensation dripped off the water bottles and onto the kitchen floor, TJ hoped she'd be able to pull it off for Marty, for Tiny, and especially for the project.

Enough thinking. She hoisted the bottles up against her chest and strolled down to where the boys were now lounging next to the creek. Marty and Rob sat with their feet in the cool, clear, running water and debated the no-rules football game that seemed to have become riddled with rules in the past decade. Tiny tossed a soggy tennis ball for Sarge to catch and drop while Scott rested his back against the massive gum tree. She felt his gaze on her as she made her way down the grassy slope toward them. It set her spine tingling pleasantly as the glittering gaze worked its way up her sun-browned legs to meet hers. Ignoring him, she handed the water around and accepted their thanks.

'Good game, guys?'

'We beat their arses.' Marty shook the water from his feet and stood up. 'How come you didn't play?'

'Uneven numbers.'

'Yeah but the oldies coulda used your help.'

'Hey! Enough of the oldies, thanks.' Rob stood up and groaned as he clutched his lower back. 'Although I might need a chiropractor tomorrow. Tiny plays a mean defence.'

'That's because you play like a girl,' responded TJ with a grin.

Rob responded by wrestling her to the ground and tickling her until she begged him to stop. Sarge wandered over and sniffed around them before giving a low growl.

'Sarge says enough, Rob. Get off me, you bully.' She shoved him up.

Rob grinned as Sarge licked his face. 'Well, at least we know he takes his job as guard dog seriously.' He rubbed the dog's ears and Sarge rolled over for a tummy pat.

TJ pushed herself up and dusted the grass off her clothes. She looked over at Scott, who leaned back with his head against the tree, his eyes closed.

'Tiny. Marty. Gather round, boys. Scott and I have something to tell you. No, it's good news,' she said as the boys looked at each other, resigned. 'In fact, it's great news. Scott?'

Scott heaved himself up and away from the tree to stand next to TJ. 'It's the best news, boys. The mayor has donated funds and labour so that we can get the asbestos removed and begin the renovations on the cabins.'

'Phwoar! That's awesome! When do we start?' Marty could hardly suppress his excitement. Out of all the boys, he was the keenest.

'For real this time, TJ?' asked Tiny, disbelief etched into his features.

TJ understood his reluctance to believe them. How many times had red tape got in their way? 'For real this time. I have the cheque and the council approval. Scott had a meeting with the mayor last week. We now have fundraising, and volunteer labour too.'

The boys high-fived each other with a whoop. 'Sweet,' they yelled in unison.

'There's more.' Her words stilled them, and their grins froze.

'Good more or bad more?' This from Marty.

'Well, that depends on you guys. Because we need to plan the renovations schedule and be available all weekend to work on the project, we've decided to set up the house as a base to work out of.' She looked from Marty to Tiny. 'So Tiny, you and Scott will be moving in here.'

'For real?' Marty beamed from ear to ear while Tiny looked a little apprehensive.

'It makes sense to us, guys. The townhouse is way too small for us, and this way you and Marty will have each other for company.' Scott reassured Tiny.

Tiny shrugged. 'I guess.'

'What about Connor and Luke?' Marty asked.

Scott looked down at TJ questioningly. She put a hand on his arm and then withdrew it again quickly when the touch felt too comfortable.

'Connor and Luke can come up and stay on the weekends if their parents agree.'

A look passed between Marty and Tiny that had the hair on the back of TJ's neck rise in warning. 'What?'

Tiny looked away and Marty scuffed his shoe against the grass as Scott asked, 'Who are Connor and Luke?'

'They're the other two boys I told you about. They're not part of the apprenticeship program but they come up here from time to time with the boys to help out around the place. Is there something we need to know, guys?'

'Nah, it's all good,' replied Marty.

TJ let it slide. 'Right. Well, we'll have to get the two spare rooms ready tonight, Marty. Scott and Tiny will be moving stuff over here from tomorrow. We can start planning once they're here and get the contractor in as soon as possible.'

'Sure thing.' Marty agreed, nudging Tiny who nodded his okay. 'Thanks, Mr D. It's cool that you went to the mayor and stuff.'

'I wouldn't have committed to this program if I didn't believe it would work. I need your commitment too.' Scott held out his hand as first Marty and then a more reluctant Tiny, shook it. 'And at home, call me Scott.'

'Now I need a word with Rob and Scott on some accounting stuff, so are you guys okay out here for a while?' At their nod, TJ turned and started up the hill leaving Scott and Rob to follow.

As soon as they reached the veranda, Rob asked, 'What's up?'

'I didn't like that look that passed between the boys at the mention of Connor and Luke. Something's going on. I had heard a rumour that Connor's parents had split but I don't know much about Luke's parents, except that his dad is a high-profile lawyer.'

'So, these are the other two gang members?' Scott lounged with a hip against the veranda railing.

'Yes. Connor is a quiet boy. He never says much when he's here. I don't think he does the hard stuff that Tiny and Marty do, but he is part of the gang and has been cautioned a few times with regards to graffiti offences. But in his case, I think it's more that he's there rather than actually participating in the activities. Luke on the other hand...' TJ swallowed around the lump in her throat. She'd longed to take him in too when he'd shown up looking like someone had used him as a punching bag.

'...is a dark horse. Often shows up with bruises, black eyes and broken bones,' Rob added.

'Abuse?' Scott frowned.

'We don't have proof. No police or hospital reports that we can find. You've met Detectives Jones and Johnson?' At Scott's nod, he continued, 'They did some research but came up blank. If it's happening like it looks, they're not reporting it.'

'And if you ask, I'm guessing he walked into a door, or broke his arm playing sport?'

TJ folded her arms protectively around herself. 'Yes, except we know that Luke doesn't play any contact sports.'

'How come they're not on the apprenticeship program?'

'Connor wants to stay at school. We can't pin Luke down to either. They come up here on invitation from the boys when they're here, and I do what I can for them.'

'I'll see what I can do. What does Ethan say?'

'Because they're not juvies, they're not on the apprentice board's radar. So, Ethan can only take a personal interest. He's tried to talk to the parents without success, apparently.'

'Judging from the look that passed between Tiny and Marty, then, you suspect they know more than they're letting on?'

'Yes. Luke Bennetti is a strange boy. Quiet, dark. Dark clothing, dark hair, always wearing long pants, hoodies and sunnies. Even on the hottest day, he won't take off his hoodie while all the others are running around with no shirts on.'

'Sounds like he's hiding something for sure. I say let them come as often as possible, and we'll work it out.'

TJ shrugged. 'I don't mind them being here. Better here than on the streets … or worse.'

Rob turned to Scott. 'I feel much better with you staying here. TJ might be capable of looking after herself, but I'm glad she has help now.'

Scott nodded. 'I'll grab Tiny now to go home and pack. There's a ton of dog food in the ute for Sarge, which I'll unload quickly. Will he be sleeping inside?'

'Yes. Unless you prefer he sleeps in a kennel outside.' TJ looked over to where the dog made his way up the grassy slope.

'At the foot of your bed would be the perfect place for him.'

TJ shivered. There was that dark velvet undertone again that made it sound like an invitation. 'Then that's where he'll sleep.'

'Right. Rob, would you like to give me a hand to unload?'

'Yeah, sure.'

TJ watched as they crossed the veranda and walked down to where Scott's ute was parked. This was it. The point of no return.

Chapter Eleven

urprisingly, things ran loudly but relatively smoothly as TJ's once quiet and peaceful home became infused with testosterone. There were boisterous fights over whose turn it was to watch their sport of choice. They set a bathroom schedule, and no one stuck to it, so most mornings, TJ would sail past, ready for work as one of the guys was pounding on the door for the other to come out.

She'd settled it by coming to an agreement with Scott that he could use her en suite to get ready for work. This meant that she had to be up at the crack of dawn to be out of her bedroom when Scott stumbled through wearing nothing but a towel.

They'd all watched from a safe distance as the last load of asbestos was lifted and removed from the property, leaving the bare wooden frames of the cabins standing like skeletons in the dying sunlight. They then celebrated with a barbeque the next day when the first load of hardwood timber cladding was delivered, and renovation could begin.

Thanks to a referral from the mayor, a local carpenter had volunteered to oversee and show the boys how to fix the cladding to the framework, and an inspector came around once a week to inspect and report.

It was as if the kiss in the kitchen had never happened. Scott kept his distance, as he'd promised, although he couldn't stop himself from watching her when he thought she wasn't looking. He told himself he was making sure that she and Tiny were getting along together, although the boy's attitude toward her had softened somewhat. Only yesterday, they'd been earnestly discussing what they were going to do next when it came to putting Sheila's engine back together.

'Happy?' he asked her now as they sat on the veranda and enjoyed the peacefulness of the cool night while the boys played a noisy video war game inside.

'It's going well, isn't it? The boys seem settled.'

'But?'

'There's a part of me that hopes we've turned a corner, but in the back of my mind, I know that Beyond Hell's Reach will come looking for Tiny soon. They won't give up that easily. No one gets to just *leave* their circle.'

Scott sighed. 'I have a feeling you're right. Let's hope we can get him well and truly back on track before that happens.'

TJ shook her head. 'I wish I could believe that's all it would take. I know something is up when they start behaving differently or don't show up for work, like Marty did. When I smell trouble, I get out on the streets at night to keep an eye on them. If I can, I intervene before they make contact, but sometimes that can have dangerous consequences for the boys.'

'Jesus, TJ. That's dangerous for you too. You're not alone in this now. Tell me if you suspect something's up, but please no more vigilante stuff on your own, okay?'

'Okay. Thanks. It would be sad for it to all go wrong now that Tiny is nominated for Apprentice of the Year.'

'Speaking of that, are you taking anyone to the awards dinner?'

TJ shrugged. 'If Rob can't make it, I normally go on my own. Why?'

'I thought we could go together if you don't have a date. No point going on our own.'

'I'm giving the two boys a lift anyway. Don't you have a date?'

Scott shook his head and drank deeply from his bottle of beer. He hadn't been interested in dating anyone since he'd met TJ and become involved in her project. Every morning, he passed her crumpled bed and imagined her lying there with that gorgeous hair spread across the pillow. Her bathroom was an eclectic mix of feminine perfumes and caustic hand cleaners to remove the grease and grime of a day's work under the bonnet. Her steel-capped work boots stood dwarfed next to his on the veranda.

She was so not his type, yet he could talk to her for hours about anything from spreadsheets to politics. And at night when he lay in his narrow bed in the room next to hers, he listened for her breathing or the sounds of her shuffling about in her bedroom and wished he could be in there with her. Then he'd remember all the reasons he couldn't and would spend the rest of the night tossing and turning until, finally, sleep claimed him.

'Well, I guess we could go as chaperones for the boys. That way we'll avoid the gossip.'

They'd done pretty well so far keeping their arrangement out of the gossip mill. For anyone who asked, it was purely a business arrangement to satisfy the mayor's requirements for supervision for the project. Mostly it was accepted. Everyone knew TJ had a strict rule about relationships in the workplace and no one dared question it. He'd quelled any murmurs in the lunch room with a stern warning.

'Perfect. Another problem solved.'

They lapsed into companionable silence again. That was another thing he liked about her. She didn't feel the need to chew his ear off. Sarge ambled out, nudging the fly screen aside to get out onto the veranda.

'Too noisy in there for you, boy?' TJ asked as he laid his head on her knee and stared at her with soppy, pleading eyes.

'I think my dog is in love with you.' Scott leaned forward with his arms on his knees and stretched out to tickle the dog's ears.

'Well, that's okay, because I'm in love with him too.' She wrapped her hands on either side the dog's jowls and kissed the permanent frown between his eyes.

'Lucky dog.' Scott leaned back again and put his feet up on the railing, crossing them at the ankles. 'Do you ever get lonely out here?'

'Never. I love the peacefulness of the valley. And there's always someone popping in to say g'day. If I do feel like company, I head on over to talk to Rose.'

'You and Mum get on well together.'

'They're the best neighbours. I love your mum. I never really knew mine. When we came to live with Pop, Nan had already passed on. I guess that explains why I was a tomboy growing up.'

'How old were you?' Scott was surprised. TJ had never shared stories about her past. In fact, he realised there was very little he did know about her at all.

'I was seven, Rob was ten, but we'd spent most of our lives in foster care until then.'

That explained her commitment to the teens, Scott thought. But what had happened to her parents? As if she'd read his mind, TJ stood, walked over to the edge of the veranda and looked out across the moonlit landscape.

'Mum died from a drug overdose not long after I was born. It took a while for the authorities to track down our immediate family. When they did, Nan was ill, and Pop was in no position to take on two young children. So, we stayed in foster care, and he visited us when he could.'

'Is that why you're so committed to this rehabilitation program?'

'Yes. I'd hate to see them travel that same path. My mother had hopes and dreams, too, until she met the man who introduced her to drugs. The rest, as they say, is history.' She seemed to realise she'd said too much. 'I'm sorry. I didn't mean to bore you with my past.'

'You're a lot of things, TJ, but you're not boring.'

'Thanks … I think.' She sat back down next to him and put her feet next to his on the railing.

'So, what's the story with your mum?' he asked.

'Do you really want to know?'

Scott was surprised to find that he did. He shrugged. 'I guess.'

She snuggled farther down in the chair and rested her head against the backrest. 'Mum ran away from home at sixteen. She worked in a pub in Melbourne, partied hard and got mixed up in the wrong crowd, according to Pop.'

She wiggled her toes against the breeze that swept

through the trees and then died away. 'Rob was born a year later. By that time, she'd cut all ties with the family, so Nan and Pop had no idea they had a grandson. By the time I came along a few years later, Mum was addicted to cocaine. She'd lost her job in the pub, had no money, and was living in a share house. Apparently one of the neighbours heard her screaming one night.'

A heavy pause fell like a weight in the silence. 'When the cops arrived an hour or so later, they found three-year-old Rob holding me wrapped in a blanket, blue around the lips, and our mother dead beside us. She'd overdosed and gone into premature labour. We were put in foster care. The rest you know.'

At a loss for words, Scott reached out to stroke her hair where it lay loose over her shoulder, a waterfall of long, silky, titian spun with gold. He twirled the strands around his fingers. 'It's a miracle you survived.'

'Yes. The police got there just in time.'

They lapsed into silence again as the noises of night peaked around them. The gentle croak of frogs from the creek ... somewhere a dog barked. How normal it all sounded. Scott's hand slipped from her hair, travelled lightly down her arm and linked with the fingers that gripped the arm of the chair tightly. He squeezed them comfortingly.

'I'm glad you're here,' he said. Then he stood up and walked inside, leaving her to her thoughts.

Friday dawned damp and gloomy as a cold front swept in. The boys grumbled as they piled into the back of the SUV — Scott's replacement for the ute. It made sense for them all to travel to work together, he'd said. It saved putting mileage on Bruce's odometer and strain on his engine. TJ wasn't about to argue. It saved her money on fuel. Bruce, bless his V8, was a bit of a fuel guzzler up the hills.

She yanked her hood up over her head and made a dash for the passenger side as Scott held the door open for her. She wished she could get rid of this feeling of foreboding that had settled in her stomach. The boys argued in the back over who'd beaten whom in their war game the night before. Scott steered the SUV down the slippery, winding road to the foothills with strong, capable hands and perfect concentration.

'You should've let me drive,' she said, pouting a little.

'I'd like to get to work in one piece thanks.' He softened his words with a smile.

'I know the road better than you in this weather. The trucks dump oil all over this road. Watch out for the patches.' She pointed to a puddle on the side of the road streaked with a layer of oil that glittered silver and blue under the dense cloud.

'I'm not driving in the emergency lane. I'm driving in the lane where I'm supposed to.'

'Just saying.'

'That constitutes back seat driving. Behave or I'll pull over and you can take the back seat.'

She folded her arms. 'City boy,' she muttered.

Scott smiled and slipped a hand from the wheel to squeeze her thigh. TJ stiffened as fire shot up through her leg and into a place she'd really rather it not go. She picked up his hand and put it back on the wheel, trying to suppress a laugh as he made to move it back to her leg again.

'At least I'm driving the speed limit and keeping my travelling distance. You'd be in and out of the traffic, weaving like a mad woman.'

'Well at least we'd get to work on time.' She looked pointedly at the hand that had returned to her leg.

He removed it with a grin. 'Just saying.'

They pulled up into the car yard parking and piled out just as the clouds parted and dumped a shower on them. Soaked to the skin, TJ skipped over puddles to unlock the door and turn off the alarm. The boys dashed past, laughing as they trailed water across the reception floor.

'One of you needs to come back with a mop and clean that up before a customer slips and falls. You've got five minutes to change, boys.'

'Sure thing, TJ. Be right back.' Surprisingly it was Tiny who responded. In the past TJ had been unable to get him to lift so much as an oil rag.

She looked up as Scott pushed through the door and

her heart stopped. His dark hair was damp from the rain as he removed his coat and shook it out. He was as gorgeous in a suit as he was in his footy gear or, for that matter, wrapped in one of her huge, fluffy pink bath towels. Her hand stilled on the booking sheet for the day as she watched him from behind the safety of the reception desk. She'd pushed those thoughts to the back of her mind so often in the last few weeks that she now allowed herself a moment to enjoy the sight.

The frown lines that had marred his brow the day they'd first met hardly appeared these days unless he was concentrating. The thunderous brows gathered only if he was really annoyed, which seldom happened now as things settled down with the change of ownership. And those eyes … those gorgeous blue eyes that now glittered with a smile rather than greyed with anger.

It was getting harder to see the boss over the man she shared her home with. Keeping them separate was even harder. Scott, the boss, was professional, fair and committed. Scott the boarder was irresistible, with charm that lured the birds from the trees — a dangerous charm becoming harder and harder to resist. Those simple touches, the odd wink, the companionship they'd fallen into as they shared a beer on the veranda at night.

He looked up and caught her looking. There it was, that devilish grin that sent her heart rocketing to her stomach and back again, bringing with it the heat that pooled in places she didn't need or want it to. Her eyes lingered on the full lips as they spoke, not hearing the words that fell from them. She watched, frozen, as he walked toward her and took her chin in his hand to tip it up. He lowered his lips to hers, touching them with a featherlight kiss before lifting his head again.

'Have a nice day, Tiger,' he whispered, pinning her eyes with his. He winked and turned to enter the corridor that led to his office.

It couldn't have lasted more than a few seconds, but TJ swore her feet were glued to the floor. Surely the soles of her safety boots had melted with the heat that surged through her at that fleeting touch of lips.

'F—'

'Fark!' Tiny whipped into the reception with the mop and almost slipped on the wet tiles. He put out a hand against the counter to stop himself falling.

'See? Now imagine if that was a customer, we'd have a compensation claim on our hands. Are you okay?' TJ recovered enough to ask.

'Yeah, no worries, mate. All good.' Tiny mopped up the wet tiles.

All good, thought TJ. Wouldn't it be nice if she could answer the same?

As the door of the workshop rolled up and the staff began to arrive, TJ wondered why she couldn't shake the feeling that something bad was about to happen. Everything seemed in order, but the feeling hung on like the grey clouds that dumped rain down until mid-morning.

By lunch time, the sun was trying to shine weakly through the gaps, and TJ's mood lifted marginally. She stepped out the back of the shop to take stock of the oil drums in the shed and noticed a black car pulled up in the staff car park to the left of the building. Tiny stood talking to someone through a dark tinted window rolled down just enough to have a conversation through.

The feeling of foreboding intensified. She tried to get the registration number, but it was too far away, so she made a note of the make and model instead. A black F-Type Jaguar, not exactly the kind of car a gangster could lie low in, but one hundred percent a car someone associated with them might drive. Like their lawyer or accountant.

A shiver ran up her spine. Surely no-one associated with Beyond Hell's Reach would be brazen enough to approach him so publicly? Tiny stepped away from the car and tipped his cap back on his head, his shoulders dragging as the driver reversed out of the parking lot.

TJ walked inside. She didn't want Tiny to think she was spying on him. Should she tell Scott? That would probably be a good idea. Her phone vibrated in her top pocket, and she pulled it out. Perfect. Detective Mark Johnson … even better.

'Hi, it's TJ.'

'Hey, staying out of trouble?' Mark chuckled in her ear.

'For now. What have you got?'

'No leads at the moment but we're working on it. Since I haven't had to go to court in the last few weeks, I'm guessing the boys are behaving themselves?'

TJ slipped into the empty office they used as a workspace for clients and closed the door. 'They were. Until a moment ago. I was just about to ring you.'

'Wait. I'll put you on speaker. Jonesy will want to know too.' Mark's voice tightened and TJ imagined him sitting up to motion his partner over to listen in. 'I'm not sure I like the sound of that.'

'No, I don't think you're going to. A black F-Type sedan was parked in the staff parking lot a few moments ago. Tinted windows, opened only enough to talk through. I couldn't see a face. It was too far away to get the registration, but it gave me a bad feeling.'

'I've learnt to trust those gut feelings. Is it the first time you've seen the car?'

'Yes, but then this is the first time Tiny has hung around for so long. I'm worried, Mark.' She gave him the year model and make of the car.

'I'll see what comes up on a cross check but it's hard without a rego. Have you spoken to Scott?'

'Not yet. I was about to.'

'Do it. I don't suppose he'd agree to security cameras in the parking lot?'

'He's as concerned as I am about the boys, so I'd say he'd definitely think about it.'

'Good. Ask him. How are you guys going shacked up together anyway?'

TJ bristled. 'We're not shacked up.'

'Aah, that says it all then. Keep an eye on those boys in the meanwhile. I'll call you if anything comes up.' With a chuckle, he hung up.

'Cheeky bastard.' TJ punched the screen to end the call. But he was right. Scott would want to know, and security cameras sounded like a good idea. It would help to curb the weekend vandalism of the used cars in the front lot too.

As she pulled open the door, Scott stood waiting at the reception desk.

'Ah, I was looking for you,' he said. 'Everything okay? Why the frown?'

'It's not good.' She held up her phone. 'I was talking to Detective Johnson.'

'Oh? And?'

'Can we talk in your office?'

'Sure.' Concern coloured his gaze as he looked down at her.

'I'll tell Tony to watch the shop. Be there in a sec.'

He nodded and went back to his office.

TJ passed Tiny on her way to talk to Tony. 'Everything okay?' He couldn't meet her eyes and her heart sank. 'You'd tell me if there was a problem, right?'

'Sure,' he mumbled and turned back to cleaning the floor.

Her heart sank farther. Gone was the smile. Gone was the happy boy he'd been the last few weeks. Something was definitely up, and she didn't need to be psychic to guess what it was. She patted his shoulder, but he turned it away. Dropping her hand she turned to give Tony instructions.

'Take care of the boys, Tony. I've got a meeting with the boss. Keep an eye on Tiny for me. We may have some trouble brewing.'

'Sure, TJ. No worries.' Tony knew the drill. 'I won't let him slip past me like Marty did the other day. I'll get him to work on Sheila for a while. He can change the battery and cables.'

'Thanks, Tony.'

She swung through the connecting door and headed down the corridor toward Scott's office. His door was open, and he held out a mug of coffee to her as she stepped through it. She took it and sipped thankfully.

'Cheers,' she said, tipping it in a toast.

He smiled back at her, and her heart did a little back flip. She should be used to that smile by now.

'So, what's troubling you?'

'A black sedan approached Tiny in the car park about ten minutes ago. Looked a little dodgy. Now Tiny's playing up. He's back to being the boy we first took home.'

'Did you see who was in the car?'

'No. The windows were tinted and only opened a crack. Just enough to talk through. I don't like it, Scott. My gut instinct tells me it's someone associated with Beyond Hell's Reach. The car reeks of money but it's too high profile to be one of the club members. They tend to stick to their Holdens, Fords, and Hemis. They don't attract too much attention that way.' She cupped the mug with her hands.

'How long did they hang around for?'

'I'm not sure. I went out to check the oil stocks and they were already there. They left a couple of minutes after.'

'Will it help if I talk to Tiny about it?'

She shook her head. 'I don't want him to think I've dobbed him in. He won't take that well at all.'

'So, what do we do?' Scott poured himself a coffee.

He stood close. A little too close perhaps, but TJ didn't move away as she normally would. The warmth he generated was comforting. She was really glad he'd come along. There was no way she could continue on this way on her own. She was tired. Tired of putting her life at risk every time the boys went off the rails, tired of shouldering the burden of the program, even when she knew she could never stop trying to help them.

She loved the boys and would do what she could, but it was getting harder to do as they got older. And the closer they got to eighteen, the more dangerous it became for them. After that, they were adults, and she had less hope of helping them at all.

When he put an arm around her shoulders and pulled her to his side, she didn't object. Instead, she lay her head against him and closed her eyes. The musky tones of his cologne teased her senses as the cashmere wool jacket tickled her nose. His hand came up to smooth her ponytail.

'Mark wants to know if you're willing to install security cameras to monitor the car park.' She should move away. Her resistance was weakening, and that could be a big mistake. But, oh for one more blissful minute, she wanted to enjoy his warm strength. 'Would you do that?'

He removed the mug from her nerveless fingers and put it down on the table next to the coffee machine. Dropping his arm from her shoulders, he placed a hand on each of her upper arms and turned her to face him. 'Yes, I will if it will help Tiny. We've come too far to lose him now.' He pulled her to him and hugged her close.

TJ sank into the solid wall of his chest and burrowed deeper into the comfort of his strength. Now was not the time to question the direction their relationship could take. She needed him. It was as simple and as complicated as that.

'Thank you.' Her voice was muffled by his jacket. She hoped she didn't have grease on her face. He'd have a problem getting that out of his Armani suit. She felt him kiss the top of her head and knew she should protest.

'I'll get the security company on to it right away.' He set her aside gently.

Reluctantly, she moved away and poured herself another coffee. She needed the caffeine. Her whole body tingled from the contact, and she was pretty sure it wasn't an allergic reaction to cashmere.

'What about Tiny?' Scott waited for a response as she took a sip from her mug.

'We'll have to keep a very close eye on him. If they're putting pressure on him, he could disappear at any time. It was going so well. This is the longest we've kept him.' The knot of muscles in her neck clenched tighter and she massaged them with her free hand.

'We won't lose him. I'll do everything I can not to.' The certainty in his reply was comforting and she hoped he was right.

'I know you will. But he turns eighteen in two days. We can't stop him from leaving after that. And his contract here is meaningless in the underworld.'

'I know. All we can do is hope that we've reached something in him to help him turn that corner.'

TJ swallowed the rest of her coffee and placed the cup on the table. 'I'd better get back to the shop. I don't want him slipping out when Tony's not looking.'

'I'll come with you and check up on the team. I

haven't been in to say hi to the guys in a couple of days. I want to do a walk around. We need to do a list of equipment and tools for the audit.'

Business as usual, exactly what they needed to return things to normal. Her moment of weakness had passed. 'I've got the tool register on my desk. Everything you need is in there.' And there was that heart-stopping smile again.

'Lead on then.' With his hand on her back, he steered her down the corridor to the workshop. He pulled the connecting door inward and held it open as she walked through it and toward her desk to retrieve the file that contained the equipment register.

He tucked it under his arm and made his round of the workshop, stopping to chat with each of the employees on the floor.

She watched as their apprehension disappeared when he talked, how he set them at ease with a joke or by showing an interest in what they were doing. After their initial concerns, they'd seen that he could be trusted. He'd proved that with his plans for improvement and a budget for new equipment. TJ had no doubt he'd deliver.

Her eyes strayed to where Marty and Tiny huddled in a corner. Marty shook his head at something Tiny said. He toed the concrete floor with his steel caps, uncomfortable with the conversation, his hands in his pockets. Time to break it up. As she neared the boys, they stopped talking but not before she heard the desperate undertone in Tiny's voice.

'I have no choice, man!'

'You do and so do I,' Marty bit back.

'Everything okay here, guys? No time for chats today. We're booked full. There is a ton of work to be done.' Her eyes pinned first one then the other.

'Getting back to it now, boss.' Marty pushed away from the wall and headed to the wash bay to turn the pressure cleaner onto the muddy four-wheel drive that stood waiting to be cleaned.

Tiny pushed past her, bumping her shoulder backwards as he walked by. The attitude was back. Her heart sank as she realised she'd been right about the occupant of the black sedan. They weren't going to leave him alone.

What had they threatened him with that left him feeling he had no choice? She could only imagine the worst as she watched Scott stride over and talk to Tiny. The boy's shoulders were rigid, eyes cast down as his body language screamed hopelessness and desperation. Scott placed a hand on his shoulder and said something in a low tone to which Tiny responded with a nod before walking away.

'He's not talking,' said Scott as he walked up to where she was standing checking off the jobs list.

'I know.'

'We'll keep a close eye on him. He'll be okay, TJ. I'll do everything I can to make sure of it.'

'I know you will. But I don't think you realise what you're dealing with. If he doesn't do what they tell him to do, they won't hesitate to get rid of him. And it won't be because he's allowed to walk away.' Desperation warred with futility.

'I really hope it won't come to that,' he said quietly.

His hand on her arm provided little comfort this time. 'Me too. But how do we stop what even the law can't?'

Chapter Twelve

As the days dragged by, Tiny withdrew and became more sullen than ever, despite their efforts to cheer him up. Whatever was happening wasn't going down in a hurry. Each day, fear seemed to grip Tiny harder. Scott wished he would talk to them, but instead he withdrew further until he no longer spoke at all, not even to Marty. He went through the daily routine without missing a beat, though, and Scott had to give him credit for that.

Tonight was the awards night, and Scott hoped that his nomination for Apprentice of the Year would cheer him a little. He was pleased to see a glimmer of a smile on his face as he and Marty stepped into the living room in their hired suits.

'You two scrub up all right.' Scott laughed as he

took in the gelled and spiked hair, gleaming shoes and slightly skewed ties.

'The ties are a killer, man. I'm choking.' Marty faked strangulation as Tiny's lips twitched.

'Try to stay alive until after dinner is served, Marty. You're allowed to remove the tie after the awards are handed out,' Scott reassured him.

'Awesome! Dunno how you wear these damn things all day.'

TJ appeared in the doorway, and Scott found himself at a loss for words. His eyes made their way up her shapely legs, and he blessed the fashion gods for those stilettos that made them go on forever. Her blue skirt swirled mid-thigh. The stiff, ruffled edges revealed far too much leg. Her bare shoulders above the strapless bodice were almost his undoing.

'Have you got something to throw over your shoulders? It's a little cool outside.'

She twirled the silver satin wrap in front of her as she stepped into the room and held it up. 'Right here.'

Taking a steadying breath, he took the silky wrap from her to drop it around her shoulders. It would be a long night sitting next to her and trying to remain neutral.

'Let's get this show on the road.' He strode out the door and down the steps to help her into the car. The problem with SUVs was that it was quite a leg up. Scott found himself closing his eyes and praying for strength as the ruffled skirt slid up her thigh. He closed the door as soon as her feet were out of harm's way.

As he walked around to the driver's side, he knew he would have trouble concentrating on driving. Perhaps he should have let one of the boys drive. It might be safer.

Thirty minutes later, he negotiated the traffic into the underground car park of the Perth Convention Centre, no less aware of her presence because of the drive. Her perfume filled the cabin, her soft voice teased his ear as she leaned around between the seats for a pep talk on etiquette with the boys. With her legs angled toward him as she turned in the seat, his hand brushed her knee every time he changed gears. And since he seldom got out of third gear in the city traffic, that was far too often for his comfort.

By the time they exited the tight confines of the lift, his forehead beaded with sweat. He could blame the stuffiness of the small space, but with TJ pressed up against him, he had to be honest. He sighed with relief as they entered the hall, and the cool blast of the air conditioning greeted him. His hand rested protectively on her hip as he steered her through the crowd.

They gave their names at the door, and an usher led them to their table. Scott was tempted to switch name tags to rearrange the table so that he sat opposite her instead of next to her, but that would be too obvious, so he sat as she started to remove her wrap from her shoulders.

'Maybe you should leave that on? It's a bit chilly in here. Can't have you catching a cold and taking a sickie.'

She draped the wrap over the back of her chair and glanced mockingly at him. 'I work in a shop that's like a wind tunnel in winter. The temperature seldom gets above 2 degrees Celsius for the whole season. I think I can handle a little air conditioning.'

She sat down next to him. The chairs were tightly packed around the table for the venue to accommodate all the guests, so TJ and Scott had no choice but to sit thigh to thigh. He felt every wiggle and shift throughout dinner as he tried to concentrate on the conversation from the other guests at their table of eight. He wondered whether she felt anything at all.

'They're about to start with the awards, Marty,' she said leaning across him to touch Marty's arm for what felt like the umpteenth time that night. 'Are you ready?'

'Yep, this is so cool.'

Scott fiddled with his tie. Cool was not how he'd describe where he was right now.

'The MTA would like to show their appreciation to the flagship dealer, Mal's Motors for their commitment to the Apprenticeship Rehabilitation Program this year. The Certificate for Commitment to Excellence is awarded jointly to Tiffany Stevens and Scott Devin as ambassadors of the program.'

Pride surged through Scott as TJ walked ahead of

him to the stage. She'd worked hard to earn the award, and if she could forget for just one moment her concerns over Tiny's safety, then this was the best diversion.

'The award for Most Improved Apprentice of the Year goes to Terence 'Tiny' Watts, who has shown commitment and endurance to his work over the last few months, achieving a 95% average on his practical tests.'

They clapped as Tiny made his way to the stage, and Scott couldn't stop his own smile spreading as Tiny's face beamed.

'And finally, we are pleased to announce that the Apprentice of the Year Award goes to Martin Petrowski.'

'Sweet,' yelled Marty as he high-fived guests on his way through the crowd.

Scott shook the boys' hands as they stood for the group photo. This must be what it felt like to be a proud father. He wondered whether TJ wanted children of her own or if she was content playing mum to her troubled teenagers.

'Ladies and gentlemen,' said the presenter as they filed back to their table, 'we hope you'll enjoy our entertainment for tonight. Dessert and coffee will be served soon. While we wait, please take to the dance floor and enjoy.'

Scott watched a few minutes later as TJ danced energetically with the boys and really wished her skirt was ankle length. Her shoulders glittered under the flashing lights. This was the first time he'd seen her let her guard down completely as she danced and laughed with first Marty, then Tiny.

Even Tiny was smiling again after a week of grunting and sombre looks. It was at times like this that Scott held out hope that they had indeed helped him turn a corner, and that the threat they thought existed for him was just the fear of losing him again. But it was TJ who held his gaze, her face alive and her body doing things in time to the music that had him shifting uncomfortably in his chair. Enough. He pushed through the crowd on the floor and stepped in between her and Marty.

'My turn, Mate.' He raised his voice to be heard over the music. Marty nodded and found someone else to dance with. The tempo slowed as Scott took her in his arms. Perfect timing. With only the slightest hesitation, she placed her right hand on his shoulder and her left hand in his.

They could do little more than sway as more people crowded the floor. He held her tightly against him, her hand anchored to his chest. The top of her head only just reached his shoulder even in those impossibly high heels. They did great things for her legs, but how did she walk on the damn things, let alone dance in them?

His arm tightened at her waist. She fit against him like a tailored glove and, this close, she'd know by now how much he appreciated it. Her eyes were fixed on his shoulder as she held herself stiffly, minimizing contact as much as possible in the cramped space. Rhythmically, he stroked her back until she relaxed in his arms.

God, that felt good. No one had ever felt as if they belonged in his arms quite like TJ did. With each brush of her body against his, he wished they were alone somewhere where they could enjoy this sensation that flowed between them.

She turned her head to meet his gaze. Her lips parted and he saw no reason to waste the opportunity as he lowered his mouth to meet hers.

Someone bumped into TJ from behind, breaking the contact. 'Sorry!'

Scott lifted his head and froze. Serena Snow stood less than a foot away, her cold glance snapping between them.

'Well, well, well! It looks like the great Scott Devin is still up to his old tricks. What did he promise you, love? A car, a house, a … raise?' Serena's words dropped loudly into the silence as the band went to announce a break. The innuendo rippled through the crowd, whipping heads in their direction. Confident that she had their attention, she eyed TJ critically. 'Not quite up to your usual standards, Scott.'

'That's enough, Serena.' Scott's voice was low but the edge in it sliced through TJ. It had no effect on Serena.

'Wait! Let me guess. She's the one heading up the

apprenticeship program and you're scoring brownie points by funding it. Or maybe she's putting out in return for a little funding.'

Scott's hands went to TJ's shoulders to move her out of the line of fire, but she dug her heels in.

'It's okay, Scott. I'll get this round.' TJ turned to face the svelte, Nordic blonde, eyeing her with the same disdain she'd dished out. Before she could speak, Marty pushed his way into the fray.

'TJ! It's Tiny. He's gone.'

'What? Where?' Anger evaporated as her stomach plummeted.

'I dunno. He said he was going to the loo, but when I went to look for him in there, he was gone.'

'Damn it!' She shoved Serena out of the way.

Scott had only a split second to enjoy the moment as Serena stumbled over a chair before TJ took off at a run. She stopped only long enough to remove her shoes as he followed closely behind.

TJ burst through the doors of the Convention Centre and out onto the paved walkway. There was no sign of Tiny.

'Give me your phone.' Manners fled as panic took hold. The sinking feeling she'd had since the black sedan had approached Tiny at work was now a full-blown churning in her stomach. She snatched the phone from Scott's hand and dialled Mark Johnson's number, putting him on speaker. 'Tiny's missing. It's going down.' Her words fell over each other in her haste to get them out.

'Tell me.' Mark thankfully didn't waste time with useless words.

'We're at the Convention Centre. He went missing about five, maybe ten minutes ago. Said he was going to the loo. I'm out looking now.'

'Is someone with you? I don't want you to go looking. Stay where you are until I get there. I'm on my way.'

TJ heard a rustle and the jangle of his keys down the line. 'Well, you'd better hurry because I'm not waiting for you to get here. Marty will be waiting for you at the entrance. Scott's with me.'

'Jesus, TJ! Can you please listen for once? You have no idea what you're dealing wi —'

TJ hung up and tossed the phone back to Scott. 'Keep an eye on Marty. I don't need him disappearing too.' She didn't hang around to see if Scott obeyed.

A quick search of the nearby train station and building alleys delivered nothing. She ran down into the basement car park. There were only two exits, so she headed for the main one. As she ran toward the security booth, she saw the tail lights of a familiar black sedan disappear through the boom gate. Too late. Her only hope now was the security camera footage which Mark would ask to see when he got there.

Scott caught up seconds later. 'Any luck?'

TJ shook her head. 'I missed them. The black sedan was here,' she puffed.

'You couldn't stop him anyway. You know that. If you had tried, they would have got you too.'

'Yes, I know that. I should've been keeping a closer eye on him.'

'You can't watch him 24/7. He's eighteen now, an adult.'

Bitterness swept through her as she remembered how they'd celebrated his eighteenth birthday and how happy he'd been. No one had ever baked him a cake before, so the red toolbox cake she'd made had gone down a treat. He'd even hugged her briefly in thanks. Now that memory lay churning in her stomach as dread replaced it in her heart.

'They'll kill him.'

'No, they won't. Come. Mark said he'd meet us upstairs.'

'Is Marty okay?' She rubbed her arms as gooseflesh crawled up them. When Scott's arm came around her, she didn't argue.

'He's safe with Tony and the others. That was quite a shove you gave Serena.' A measure of pride edged his voice as he guided her to the stairwell.

'Oh, God! Is she really pissed at me? I didn't mean to shove so hard.'

Scott considered for a moment. 'I think it's fair to say you have a few more admirers amongst the MTA members tonight. I think there were a few of them who would have done the same.'

TJ smiled through the pain in her heart. 'She's got a mean mouth on her.'

'Unfortunately, I don't think we've heard the end of it either.' He let go of her shoulders to slide a hand down her arm and take her hand to help her up the steps. 'Your feet must be sore after that sprint.'

She grimaced. 'A little tender, but nothing a good soak won't fix when we get home.' It sounded so intimate, so normal. But they'd be going home without Tiny.

'Want me to carry you?'

She laughed. 'I'm not a princess, Scott. I can walk just fine, thanks.' Even if she was limping a little.

They walked out of the stairwell to where Mark stood interviewing witnesses. He spotted them and swiftly finished his round of questioning to meet them halfway.

'Any luck,' he asked.

TJ shook her head. 'But there should be something on video surveillance.'

'I've got one of the guys looking into it now for us. If he can get a clear look at the registration plate, he'll run a check, but my guess is they'll be stolen or masked plates. You okay?'

TJ nodded. 'I'm fine.' Marty came over with her shoes and wrap. 'Thanks, mate.'

Scott placed the wrap around her shoulders as she continued to hold her shoes.

'We'll find him, I promise,' said Mark.

'I know you will. I hope you find him before it's too late.'

'We'll do our best. Go home now. I'll call you as soon as we have something.'

TJ nodded, but her stomach churned as a cold chill crept up her spine. She rubbed her arms as Scott led her and Marty back down the stairs to the car.

'What's going on, Marty,' she asked as Scott turned the key in the ignition. 'You won't get into trouble, and we won't let anything happen to you. If you know where he's gone or who he's with, you really need to tell us.'

'I swear I don't know. I told Detective Johnson everything I know. Tiny told me this guy had come to see him at work. He didn't give me a name, only said it was an old guy.' Marty paused as his breath hitched. 'He wanted Tiny to do a run for him. Tiny told him no.'

'So, what happened tonight?'

'Like I told you, he said he was going to the loo. He never said anything else, I swear. He didn't run away, TJ. He didn't arrange this.'

'It's okay. I believe you. What was with the look between you two when I mentioned Luke and Connor coming to stay a couple of weeks back?'

Marty sighed. 'It's just a feeling we have. About Luke's dad.'

'What about Luke's dad?' Scott prompted.

'Well, you know how Luke's always got bruises and stuff? His mum does too. Everyone knows his old man has a temper, but there's something else too. Like he's dodgy, you know?'

'Dodgy how?'

'We think he might be a dealer.'

'Jesus, Marty … have you told Detective Johnson that?' TJ spun around to face him where he sat in the rear between the two front seats.

'No. If he is and they find out I've dobbed, I'm dead.'

'Is that who you think might have come to take Tiny tonight?'

'Jeez, I dunno, TJ.'

A thought struck harder than a lightning bolt. Would a crime boss be that arrogant though? Quite possibly, if he thought he was untouchable. 'What car does Luke's dad drive?'

'A black one, I think. A Jag, maybe?'

His words fell like a ton of rock into the sudden silence.

It took a while for everyone to settle when they arrived home. Scott removed his suit jacket and lit the fire in the stone fireplace. The peaceful flicker of the flames warmed the cold lounge room.

He settled into the armchair that stood beside it as TJ curled up on the couch. Sarge wandered in to curl up next to Marty on the floor where he sat with his back against the couch and TJ's comforting hand on his shoulder. Silence stretched between them as they all reflected on the events of the night in the soothing glow of the fire. Marty wandered off to bed around midnight with a solemn promise to TJ that he wouldn't run away too.

'I'm done with it, I swear. I wish Tiny was too.' He disappeared through the door into the corridor to his room.

'Coffee?' TJ sat up to swing her legs to the floor.

'Good idea.' Scott picked up his discarded jacket off the arm of the chair.

'I'm not sure I'll be able to sleep until we find Tiny.'

'Why don't we change into something more comfortable? I think we're in for a long night.' He stood up and stretched.

She rubbed Sarge's ears, sending him into a blissful state as he stared at her adoringly. 'If I was in a different mood, I could take that as an invitation.' She tried hard to lighten the mood, but her head was filled with thoughts of all the awful things Tiny might be going through right now.

'At any other time, it would be. Right now, coffee

and PJs sound like exactly what we need. Off you go, I'll put the kettle on.'

'It's okay. I'll get it. I think your suit is more uncomfortable than my dress.'

She put the kettle on and set out the mugs before following him up the corridor to change into her not-so-sexy, boringly decent pyjamas. As she passed the boys' bathroom, she heard the shower running. With Scott taking a shower in there rather than her en suite, it would give her back her own space and a little more time to think about who might have taken Tiny.

Warm on the outside, numb on the inside, she returned to the kitchen to spoon instant coffee into their mugs, her mind playing out all the scenarios she did and didn't want to see. When Scott came into the kitchen, she held out the steaming mug of coffee. He took it gratefully, wrapping his hands around the mug. He followed her back into the lounge where they sat side by side on the couch, sipping silently on a brew that tasted nothing like the coffee that came from his machine.

'That was quite a scene Serena caused,' TJ said after a while.

'I'm sorry she was so rude to you. I had no idea she'd be there.'

TJ shrugged. 'She picked the perfect moment to stage her little drama.'

'Yes. She's good at that.'

'Will her showing up here cause trouble for you with the press?'

'It might. I'll ring my lawyer tomorrow for advice. I'm more concerned about the focus it might bring to the program. All it needs is for an ambitious reporter to pick up on the negative side of the program and bring all we've achieved so far crashing down around our ears. Especially with Tiny missing again.'

'That's what I'm afraid of.' TJ tucked her legs up under her and twisted to face him, resting her head against the back of the couch. She propped her empty mug on her knees. 'God, I hope he's okay. I just have this really sick feeling.'

Scott leaned over to take her mug from her nerveless fingers and put both his and hers on the coffee table next to the couch. He reached over and entwined his fingers with hers as they lay in her lap. Gently, he squeezed her fingers. Since she'd echoed the feeling that had settled in his own gut, he said nothing.

When a tear slipped down her cheek, he raised their joined hands to wipe it away. He tugged her closer until she sat curled up against him with his arm cradling her close as she cried for the boy they'd lost. Most likely forever this time.

Chapter Thirteen

TJ stretched against the warm, firm body beneath her. Her hand stilled in its mission as it crept up the strong cords of a neck and stubbly chin. Her eyes popped open. Frozen, she realised she lay sprawled over Scott with her head tucked under his chin. Carefully, she attempted to roll off him and fell off the couch, squarely on her arse.

'Shit! Ouch.'

Scott flipped out his hand, palm up, his chuckle annoyingly sexy. '20c for the swear jar.'

'Put it on my tab,' she answered grumpily.

'Not comfortable enough for you, Tiger?'

Perhaps a little too comfortable, but she wasn't about to admit to that. She glared at him as he turned his head to look at her. Sarge got up from in front of the fire to flop down next to her and lay his head in her lap. As the sleep haze receded, she remembered.

'Marty! Sorry, boy.' Nudging Sarge away, she leapt up. Outside Marty's room, she stopped to take a breath before knocking. 'You awake, Marty?'

'Yeah.'

The sound of his feet hitting the floor followed his sleepy drawl. TJ released the breath she'd been holding. He'd stayed. He hadn't run away to follow Tiny.

'Sweet. I'm going to make coffee and toast for breakfast. Be ready in fifteen minutes.'

'Yep, sure, TJ.'

She turned away from his door to see Scott leaning against the wall.

'Everything okay?'

'For now.' Fully awake, the reality hit once more. They'd been holding on to a false sense of security the whole time. The fight to protect her boys from the underworld would never end. Dealers would keep dealing. Suppliers would keep supplying. And they would keep targeting the kids who were the most vulnerable. The ones looking for a good time, believing they couldn't have one without being on a high. Or the ones who felt like outcasts and were just looking for a place to belong. Rob was right. She couldn't save them all.

'Don't lose hope, TJ. Not now.' Cupping her face with his hands, he kissed her forehead.

'I should be out there looking for him.'

Scott shook his head. 'That's a job for the police. As hard as it is, there's nothing you can do for Tiny now that won't put you or Marty in danger yourselves. Let the cops handle it.'

'I can't stay here and do nothing.'

'You are doing something. You're here for another boy who needs you. Now more than ever with his mate in trouble. For Marty's sake, go and freshen up. Have a shower, clear your head. I'll make breakfast then we can sit down and work through the logistics. Figure out what we know that might help your detective find Tiny.' With his arm around her shoulders, Scott steered her up the corridor to her room. 'Take your time. Marty and I will be here waiting for you.'

Half an hour later, they sat in silence around the kitchen table. TJ checked her phone again for what seemed like the hundredth time. Still no word from Tiny or the police. She dialled Tiny's number, but it rang out. Her head hurt from thinking about all the things he might be going through. A shower couldn't wash the dread away. With a sigh, she dropped the phone on the table and sipped her coffee.

The brew was strong enough to put hair on her teeth, but it gave her the zing she needed. She looked across the table to where Scott scrolled through the screen of his phone, absorbed in the news of the day, the way he'd done every morning since moving in. How could he be so calm when her own nerves were stretched to breaking point?

Sensing her stare, he looked up from his screen. 'Problem, Tiger?'

His voice slid over her like dark, smooth, liquid chocolate. She closed her eyes and let the sensation flow over her to soothe her rigid spine and relax her knotted neck muscles as surely as if it was his hands doing the soothing. Opening her eyes, she stood to clear the breakfast dishes from the table. 'Nope. No problem.' She turned to stack the plates in the dishwasher.

The sound of a chair scraping back on the wooden floor made her jump, the knot in her stomach tightening.

'Marty, can you go across to Bill's and let him know we're going to be laying the floorboards in Cabin One today? He said he'd bring over his new circular saw for us to use.' He spoke to Marty, but she could feel his eyes burning between her shoulder blades.

'Sure can. Gives me something to do other than think about Tiny.' Relief coloured the boy's tone as Marty slipped out the kitchen door.

TJ felt rather than heard Scott behind her as her nerve ends screamed. 'I can't stop thinking the worst this time.' She turned into his arms.

'I know it's hard, TJ, but you can't give up hope.' He placed his hands on her hips to draw her closer.

Her palms traced his forearms up to his shoulders, his skin warm and the muscles firm beneath her hands. Touching him grounded her. She let them come to rest against the beat of his heart, the steady rhythm soothing. 'Thank you for standing with me. Mal Malone wouldn't have done what you're doing.'

'I'm not Mal Malone.'

'No, you're not.' TJ reached up to cup his face and bring his head down to hers. She kissed him, softly, sweetly, with all the emotion she'd been bottling up since he'd breezed into their lives and changed it for the better.

He returned her kiss, taste for taste, gently increasing the pressure until she relaxed in his arms and gave herself up to the sensations that coursed through her. Gentle hands at her waist lifted her up onto the kitchen bench top as he moved to stand between her legs. She hooked them around his waist and shifted closer, needing his solid strength.

Her hands strayed to unhook the buttons on his shirt and push it aside. The feel of his heated skin against her hand sent a shiver through her. She eased her lips from his and placed them against the cord that pulsed in his neck, absorbing the beat of his heart as it drummed through her. His hands played rhythmically up and down her back with a gentle motion that sent trails of fire in its wake.

A car door slammed and set Sarge barking madly on

the veranda. With a sigh, Scott straightened and lifted her off the bench. He cradled her against him for a second or two longer. 'Hold that thought for later, Tiger.' At Sarge's warning growl, he gently set her aside. 'Whoever it is, Sarge doesn't recognise them. Stay here. I'll go and check.'

'TJ?' A voice called up from the driveway below the veranda. 'Can you call your monster off, please?'

She breathed out slowly. 'It's Mark. He must have news. Stand down, Sarge,' she ordered as she stepped through the door.

Mark's face was grim as he stepped onto the wooden boards. TJ's hand flew to her mouth, covering the strangled sound that slipped from her throat as her world crumpled at her feet. She shook her head at the look in his eyes, knowing in her heart, before he even spoke, that her worst nightmare had come true.

'I'm sorry, love. We found him in a toilet block along the river.'

The weight of Scott's arm settled around her shoulders as he drew her in to his side. For a moment, she buried her head in his chest. Pain seared through her heart as sharp as a knife. Tiny was gone.

'Overdose?' Scott held TJ tightly against him. One hand stroked her hair, the other stroked her back as he directed the question at Mark.

'Jonesey is down there waiting for the coroner to confirm it, but it looks that way.'

'And the black sedan?'

'Masked plates, as we suspected. The dark tint on the windows made it impossible to see who was driving or if there was anyone else in the car. Even the windscreen shot was no good. The driver was wearing a wide brimmed hat and kept his head down.'

'Bastards.'

'I can't tell you much right now. We can't afford to reveal anything that might compromise the case. But I will make you a promise, TJ, and that promise is I *will* find out who did this to Tiny.'

TJ's head jerked up. 'What about Marty? Will he be safe?' She pushed against Scott's chest until he let her go. Tears glittered in her eyes.

'I don't believe Marty is a target. He was a user, and not in as deep as Tiny was.'

TJ looked over Mark's shoulder to where Marty, Bill and Rose came up the drive. They laughed and joked happily together with Bill ruffling Marty's hair and delivering a few mock jabs. It broke her heart that what she had to tell them was about to destroy that tenuous thread of joy.

As if sensing the tension in the air, Marty stilled his sparring with Bill and dropped his hands to his side. His eyes darted between the TJ and the detective.

'TJ?' When he saw the tears on her cheeks, his voice hitched.

TJ tried to speak but the words lodged behind the lump in her throat. She looked up at Scott.

'They found Tiny,' he said, quietly.

'Where is he? He's okay, right?'

Scott shook his head. 'I'm sorry, Marty. They found him too late.'

Marty hung his head and booted the gravel at his feet. 'Fuck these people! I warned him. I told him it was a bad idea to go back. I told him he'd get hurt for real this time.' His voice broke on the words as he spun around and ran down to the creek.

'Sarge, follow!' Scott commanded.

Marty stopped and waited for the dog to catch up, putting a hand on his collar when Sarge nudged his hand.

Rose stepped forward to take charge. 'Come, TJ. I'll make us a nice cup of tea.' She took TJ's hand and patted it between hers. 'Let's go inside, love.'

'I can't let Marty out of my sight.' Her throat hurt, her head pounded, and the ache of loss weighed on her heart. 'I can't lose him too.'

'Scott and Bill will keep an eye on him. Then we'll come out and sit on the veranda where we can see him.'

TJ nodded and let Rose lead her inside. Emotions hammered at her as they walked up the steps. Guilt, regret, hopelessness. 'I let him slip away, Rose.'

'No, you didn't, love. He made his own choices.'

'If I'd been watching him, he wouldn't have slipped

out. I would have seen him go. I could have followed him. Instead, I was …' TJ remembered vividly what she had been doing.

'You were what? Enjoying yourself for a change? Letting your hair down? Having fun instead of worrying about everyone else? There's nothing wrong with that.'

TJ shook her head, disbelief clouding what she'd suspected in her heart from the start. 'Tiny was really happy here. He'd turned a corner. He wouldn't have gone with them willingly.'

'Mark will get to the bottom of it.'

'But it won't bring Tiny back.'

'No, it won't. But you still have Marty, Luke and Connor to think of. And all the others who will come after. You can try but you can't save them all, love. That's the sad reality of what you're trying to do.'

TJ sighed as she stepped through the door into the kitchen and flipped the switch on the kettle. Her movements mechanical, born of habit, as she reached for mugs from the cupboard and took teabags out of the jar. Mundane tasks that made their world keep turning when a young life had been cut short.

'What if the mayor pulls the funding on the building project? Then they have nothing. Still nowhere to go.'

'Scott will make sure that doesn't happen. You're not alone in this anymore. Besides, the community has already had a taste of volunteering for the project. They've come to believe in it as much as you have.

They'll be behind you this time because they've seen for themselves that it works.'

'It didn't work for Tiny. I feel as if I've lost control, Rose.' TJ dropped the spoon in the mug with an angry splash. She turned around and folded her arms.

Rose stepped forward and pulled her into a hug. 'No, you haven't. What happened with Tiny is all the more reason you need to get the shelter up and running. Come on, TJ. Where's that fighting spirit we love so much. You can't give up. For Marty's sake, if not your own. Has Marty run away again? No, he hasn't. He had the opportunity, and he didn't take it. That's because of you.' She thumbed the tears from TJ's cheeks. 'Now, finish making that tea before it gets cold.'

TJ nodded and turned back to the bench. 'I'll take a cup down to the creek for Marty and have a chat with him.'

'You do that, love. I'll finish up here. Did you want Bill or Scott to go with you?'

'No,' TJ replied, shaking her head. 'I'll take care of it.'

The mugs seemed to weigh a ton in her hands as she willed her feet to move. She heard Mark's car drive away with a sinking feeling that things were going to get a lot worse before they would get better. The sound of Scott's voice coming closer spurred her on. She didn't want to face him right now. What had happened to Tiny was yet another reason why she couldn't become involved with anyone. The moment she turned her back, something bad happened. She detoured through the lounge room and out through the French doors that led to the opposite side of the veranda to avoid him. If Rose thought that was strange, she didn't say a word.

Marty sat against the old gum tree, head back, eyes closed with his fingers stroking the dog's fur gently. Sarge lay close to his side, his ears twitching as he tuned in to the sounds around him.

'Hey,' said TJ, holding the mug out to Marty.

'Hey.' The response was tired, deflated. He reached up to take the mug from her nerveless fingers.

She sat down next to him and ruffled Sarge's ears. 'You okay?'

Marty shrugged. 'I guess. It sucks, TJ.'

'I know. We'll find out who did this. With or without Mark's help. That's a promise.'

'It's too dangerous. We're better off forgetting it. No one messes with these guys. Tiny didn't OD. He disobeyed an order, and they killed him.'

'We don't know that for sure yet, Marty. We have to wait for the coroner's report.'

'No! They made it look like suicide. They came to work looking for him to do a run. He said no. He told them he was out and getting clean. They threatened him. He was scared. He wanted me to come with him, shadow him, so that if something happened there was a witness, but I was too scared after what happened last time. I don't want to die, TJ. I'm happier now than I've ever been. Tiny was too.'

'So why did he leave the function then?'

'I don't think he left on his own. He really did go to the dunny. I think they were waiting for him.'

'The perfect setting to take him. It makes sense, I guess. A lot of people milling around. No one would really notice more black suits coming and going.'

'I should have gone with him.'

'Then you would both be gone. Promise me something?'

'Yeah?'

'Please don't run away again? No matter what it is, I want you to come to me. If you can't speak to me, please speak to Scott. Promise?'

Marty nodded as TJ stood up and held out her hand for his mug. He swallowed his tea and handed it to her. 'Promise.'

Chapter Fourteen

Scott was in a foul mood. He'd spent the last half hour on the phone convincing the mayor not to withdraw the funding for the project. Tiny's death had been ruled as an accidental overdose. There'd been insufficient proof for the coroner to rule otherwise, which made Scott wonder whose payroll the coroner was on.

With an election coming up, the mayor was terrified of bad press. Scott managed to convince him that there was no ongoing danger to the community, but it had been hard work.

He was tired. Since Tiny's death, neither he nor TJ had had much sleep. At night he'd hear her moving quietly around the house. Every creak of the floorboards made him want to get up and go to her. But he couldn't.

She'd put up a solid wall between them. Now that

Tiny was gone, there was no reason for him to stay on at the house, but TJ hadn't asked him to leave yet either. Maybe she would after the funeral.

He didn't want to leave. He loved the house, the land, the feeling of peace … and he loved being with TJ. His life was so different here.

The office door opened, and his heart leapt in his chest. It sank again as he realised it was Serena, not TJ, who stepped through the door.

'What do you want?'

'Oh, come now, Scott. That's not the way to greet an old friend.'

Scott didn't bother to reply that she was the last person he'd consider a friend as she sashayed over to his desk. She perched on the edge, her skirt lifting to mid-thigh and showing an expanse of shapely leg. He sat back in his chair and glared at her. To his annoyance, she laughed. The sound skittered along his nerve ends and set his teeth on edge. 'Don't make me call my lawyer, Serena. You're in breach of your AVO. Twice in one week.'

'I came to apologise for causing a scene at the dinner last week. I realised that you have a lot more on your plate than a new staff member to harass. Drugs, dealers, suicides.'

'It's none of your business. Get out.' He reached for his phone.

'That could get very messy for you, Scott.'

'I'm going to remind you of this one more time before I call the cops. You're in breach of your restraining order.' He stood up to tower over her. 'Get out.'

She slid off the desk and adjusted her skirt as she came closer. 'You don't expect me to take that seriously do you? A girl does what it takes to survive in this world.'

'And you take things a little too far. Now get out.'

She stepped up and stood close, running a manicured nail down the row of buttons on his shirt. 'There was a time when you enjoyed that.'

'More fool me.' His hands covered hers to push them away. 'I don't know what you came here for, Serena, but whatever scheme you're cooking up in your head … forget it.'

She pouted in a way he'd once found attractive. Now it annoyed him.

'Oh, I think you underestimate me. I'm sure the media will be thrilled to hear of your latest escapades.' She sidled closer as her arms crept up around his neck. 'Living with one of your female employees, harbouring drug runners who turn up dead after receiving a coveted award? Great fodder for the press.'

He placed his hands on her hips to push her away. 'Your threats don't scare me.'

She stretched up against him, her lips inches from his. 'Well, they should. I can make your life hell.'

'And once again, I think the ball is in my court here because I'm not the one in breach of a court order. You are. So, you might want to get your claws out of my neck.' He met with resistance as he pushed her away.

Whatever she meant to say next was lost as with a soft knock, TJ entered the office. The surprise on her face was followed by a mocking look in her eyes. 'I'm so sorry to interrupt your little reunion. When you're done here, Scott, I need you to sign off on Tiny's file so I can submit it to the apprentice board.'

Scott shoved a little harder at Serena, wishing he could wipe the self-satisfied smile off her face. The intent in her eyes spoke loudly to a set up. She'd been hoping someone would walk through the door and misunderstand what they saw.

'I can tell you're a little busy right now. Come and see me when your ... guest ... has left.'

As TJ turned and left the office, closing the door behind her, Scott shoved Serena away, not caring if she fell flat on her conniving arse. If she wanted to sue for that too, she was welcome to try.

'Get out!' Picking up his phone, he dialled the number for the local police station. When the constable answered, he said, 'I'd like to report the breach of a restraining order please.'

Serena's eyes narrowed on his as she stood. 'You'll pay, Scott. One way or another.'

'You've cost me enough already.' To the officer on

the other end of the line he gave Serena's details. 'She has two minutes to leave the premises before I take action.' He paused to hear the officer's response. 'Thank you.' Quietly he put the mobile phone down on his desk. 'They're on their way.'

Without a word, she turned to leave, smashing the office door against the frame behind her. Scott took a deep breath. His hands were shaking. Not because he was afraid of her threats but because he'd been so angry he'd wanted to throttle her.

It had taken all his restraint not to throw her out, but she would have used that against him in court, even when she had instigated contact. Disgust tasted sour in his throat at how the scene must have looked to TJ when she'd walked into the office.

He stepped over to the window to make sure she left and saw Serena talking to TJ on the driveway. Serena Snow was the kind of woman who delighted in trampling over anyone in her path in her expensive Jimmy Choos. And TJ looked like she was ready to swing anything she could get her hands on. Scott strode to the door and whipped it open.

'You're just another notch on his bedpost, you do realise that don't you?'

TJ stiffened as the cold, shrill voice lanced through

her. She straightened from under the bonnet of the car she was checking the oil and water levels on. Taking her time, she turned to meet Serena's narrowed eyes full on. She shivered at the meanness that lurked in the silvery gaze. 'I have no idea what you're talking about.'

'Quite the little plain Jane when you're not all dressed up. Don't think I don't know what your game is. Oh, you might think you're clever now, but wait until he drops you like a hot potato when someone more ...' Serena's insulting gaze travelled from TJ's worn boots, up over her grease-stained overalls to her tangled hair bunched into an elastic band, '... interesting and attractive comes along.'

'Thanks for the advice.' There was no point telling her that they weren't sleeping together. Serena was in no mood to hear the truth. 'I'll try to remember that when we're having hot, sweaty sex on my sofa.'

'You little ... cat!'

TJ blocked the swing of Serena's arm, catching the woman's thin, bony wrist with her hand. 'The word you're looking for is bitch. You really don't want to hit me.' With the other hand, she lifted the wrench from inside the engine bay and slipped it into her pocket, enjoying the fleeting fear that crossed Serena's face. 'I fight dirty.'

'The cops are on their way. I'll tell them you threatened me.'

'Go ahead ... but my suggestion would be that you

get back in that car and leave before the police run a plate check and find out who it really belongs to. You're on my turf now. You made a very stupid move coming here today. There's a lesson to be learnt from digging holes for people, Serena. Be careful you don't fall in one yourself.'

'You have no idea what you're talking about.' She moved forward threateningly. In her heels, she was a few inches taller than TJ.

'Try me.' Around Serena's shoulder she saw Scott push through the doors and walk toward them. In the opening to the workshop, her team stood waiting for a sign to rush in and help. The red and blue lights of the police car flashed as it turned into the drive and TJ added, 'If I were you, I'd go quietly and maybe the cops won't ask questions. With a bit of luck, they won't recognise the car or the driver. But I wouldn't count on it.'

Serena's eyes narrowed. 'Watch your back. Or you could end up like that boy.' The sneer turned what might have once been a pretty face into a monster's as Scott moved in beside TJ.

'Is that a threat or a confession?' TJ smiled and waved to the officers as they got out of the car. Serena pushed past her, nudging her shoulder hard as she swept by.

'I'm going.' She got into the black car and backed out to drive away.

Scott placed his hand on her arm. 'Are you okay?'

'I'm fine.' Her hand shook a little, shock mixing with anger. 'She's out for blood.'

'I know. I thought she'd go away after the court case. I guess I was wrong. There has to be an ulterior motive for her showing up here. Serena never does anything without a motive.'

'Seems like an awful lot of nastiness in return for unrequited love.'

'She's ambitious. It's about money and trophies. Love doesn't come into it at all.'

'You must be quite a catch.'

He smiled at that. His heart-stopping, dimpled smile that curved those firm lips into a sexy upward curve and invited fingers to touch them. 'Only for the right person.'

TJ's heart thumped as heated blue eyes seared into hers, their message unmistakable. Yes, he would be a good catch. Just not for her. She said nothing as the policemen approached them.

'Hey, TJ,' the young constable greeted. 'I see the lady left.'

'Yes, Tim, although I'd use the term *lady* loosely. You might want to run the plate number on the car though. I think she's got herself into some nasty company.' She repeated the vehicle registration number for him.

Tim nodded and looked at Scott. 'Mr Devin? Do you want to press charges?'

'I'll talk to my lawyer first. If you could please record the incident and note that she was in breach of her restraining order by coming here? I'm not sure pressing charges will stop her.' He looked back at TJ. 'Who was in the car with her?'

'Gino Bennetti, a lawyer with a questionable record and Luke's father. I've been doing a little research. He's not opposed to slinging mud or manufacturing evidence to win a case. Rumour has it he has strong ties to the underworld, and a few judges on his payroll.'

'We'll check it out, TJ,' promised Tim. 'Now what about you? She shoved you pretty hard.'

TJ shrugged. 'I won't press charges unless she decides to carry out her threat.'

'She threatened you?' Scott took her by the shoulders and turned her around to face him.

'She told me to watch my back. Not much of a threat.'

'And she meant it. Serena doesn't play by the rules.'

TJ stepped back so that his hand fell to his side. 'Neither do I.'

'Let me know if you change your minds.' The constable looked from one to the other. 'If it's all okay here, we'll move on. I'll check that plate.'

'Thanks, Tim. You might want to pass the details on to Detective Mark Johnson too. Miss Snow made some threats that might impact on the investigation into Tiny Watts' death. I'll report those to him myself.' Scott reached out to shake the constable's hand. 'Thank you for responding so quickly.'

'Sure thing.' Tim and his partner turned to leave.

'My office. Now,' ordered Scott as they pulled out the driveway.

TJ looked up at him. 'What for?'

'I want to know exactly what Serena said to you.'

'Go to hell, Scott.'

He stopped her with a hand on her arm as she went to sweep past him into the workshop. 'Later. First, we need to sort this out.'

'There's nothing to sort out. What you do need to decide though, is exactly where your loyalties lie.'

'What the hell is that supposed to mean?' His voice was low, a growl between them that raised the hair on the back of her neck and sent shivers down her spine.

She stepped up so that they stood toe to toe, the tips of her dusty boots a strong contrast to his highly polished, expensive leather shoes. 'You and Serena looked pretty cosy when I walked into your office. How do I know this isn't something the two of you are cooking up together? You didn't seem to be fighting too hard.'

'You're wrong. I know how it must have looked but I'm not prepared to discuss it standing on the driveway with the whole dealership looking on.'

TJ looked around and saw that they'd attracted attention from the staff. Gossip was the last thing they all needed. She sighed and stepped back. 'Give me five minutes to clean up.'

Scott nodded and walked away leaving her to take several deep, calming breaths as faces disappeared from windows and went back to work. Whichever way they looked at it, their situation had just got a whole lot worse. Serena's appearance would bring a lot of unwanted attention to Scott and, in turn, to the project.

The circumstances of Tiny's death already threatened the program as the media started asking questions. It wouldn't be long before the mayor would rethink his involvement too. But whatever happened next, her commitment to Marty had to remain strong. She wasn't about to lose him too.

Serena's arrival had not been timed well. Or then again, perhaps it had. TJ realised she'd been leaning a little too much on Scott. She'd become too used to having him around. Too used to hearing him moving around in the room next door, seeing things like his aftershave and soap in her bathroom. Too used to the scent of him lingering in her bathroom after his shower.

His very being had slowly permeated her property. Little things, like the tools he'd left in the shed when he'd tinkered under Bruce's bonnet. His work shirt that hung on the hook in Cabin One, covered in sawdust. And, of course, his dog, Sarge, who was there ready to welcome them home every night, hyped up and keen to play. Like a real family. TJ realised it was the happiest she'd been since Pop died.

But there was no point in chasing windmills. Scott might be easy to talk to and great company, but their worlds were poles apart. A relationship would be a disaster. Why that thought sent a sharp burst of pain through her chest, she didn't want to guess.

Irritated, she tossed the rag she'd wiped her hands on in the recycle bin and walked up the corridor to Scott's office with purposeful strides. It had to end now.

Scott stood looking out his office window across the hills as she swept into the office. He didn't turn around as she slammed the door behind her.

'Easy on the door, Tiger. It's taken a bit of punishment today.'

He bunched his fists into his pockets. With his jacket off, TJ had a view of his broad shoulders that tapered down to a strong, muscled back that she'd seen ripple in the sunlight with each swing of a hammer, each slide of a wood saw every Saturday for the last couple of months.

To follow his comment up with a humorous response would be too easy, so she bit her lip. She needed to stay mad at him. 'What do you want, Scott? I've had enough friendly chit chat today.'

He turned from the window to face her as he leaned

up against the sill. 'It wasn't what you thought you saw.'

'I don't care. Whatever.' TJ jiggled her hand in the air, waving the problem away.

'I'm going to tell you anyway.'

'I don't have time for this. It doesn't matter to me who you have an affair with as long as it doesn't impact my project. I'm not losing any more of my boys. If the media gets hold of what happened here today, it's all over for me, for Mal's Motors and my boys.'

'Whatever was between Serena and me is over. I have no interest in rekindling it, and I'm certainly not interested in playing her games. What I want to know is what she said to you out there on the driveway. I saw her swipe at you.'

TJ shrugged. 'It doesn't matter. She didn't connect. I'm a big girl. I can take care of myself.'

'I don't doubt that for a minute.'

He smiled as he pushed away from the window. TJ's mind filled with a vision of a stalking panther as he walked casually toward her. She took a step back.

'If we're done here, I have work to do.'

Scott sighed. 'We're not done with this, but I guess it will have to wait until you're in the mood to discuss it. I won't let her hurt you or the project. That's my promise.'

'Fine. Keep her away from me. That's all I ask.' She stepped back toward the door.

'I spoke to Mark about the arrangements for Tiny's funeral.'

TJ stopped, backing up as tears surged into her eyes. She blinked them away. 'And?' The words came out a whisper as the air between them hummed with tension.

'The coroner will release him to us on Friday. So, I'll arrange the funeral for Saturday.'

Unable to force the words past the lump in her throat, TJ nodded, the reality of it beyond her grasp. Everything she'd worked for with Tiny was lost. She'd failed to tame the tiger that had Tiny in its grasp. She couldn't afford to do the same with the remaining three, especially Marty. Quietly she turned and left the office.

Chapter Fifteen

A watery sun broke out between heavy clouds and filtered in through the stained-glass window of the chapel. Scott, TJ and Marty sat close together on the front pew as the celebrant read a blessing for Tiny. Behind them, a small group of mourners spread out across the pews.

How sad that it had come to this. If only she'd kept a closer eye on him that night, maybe … just maybe … she could have prevented this. A tear slipped down her cheek and splashed on her hand. She wiped it against her skirt. Scott's hand curled around hers as it lay between them, giving it a comforting squeeze.

Surprised she had any tears left to cry, TJ dabbed her cheeks with the tissue she'd scrunched up in her free hand. Scott placed her hand on his thigh to draw her closer with his arm around her shoulders. Too drained to resist, she leaned her head against his shoulder. He brushed a kiss against her hair as the celebrant finished the reading and the coffin slipped quietly through the doors of the chamber where Tiny would spend his last moments before cremation.

Next to her, Marty's shoulders shook quietly. She stretched out her free hand to hold his, the three of them finding comfort in each other. TJ wasn't sure how long they sat like that. After a while the celebrant touched Scott's shoulder.

'I'm sorry, Mr Devin. Tea is being served outside. Please join the others when you're ready.'

'Of course, thank you.' He hugged TJ quickly before removing his arm from around her shoulders. 'Let's go, guys.'

He held out his hand to her and she took it without hesitation. Marty walked beside them as they emerged into light drizzle. Tea and cake were being served under the gazebo in the chapel garden. Scott found TJ a seat and went to get her a cup of strong coffee.

'Thanks,' she said, taking it from him with shaky fingers.

'No worries. Will you be okay here for a while?'

She nodded. 'Yeah. Thanks, Scott. For everything.'

'I'll be back.'

His smile was soft and gentle. Not the heart-stopping, cheek-creasing smile, but a smile she wished he'd deliver against her lips. The smile she imagined he saved for warm, velvety nights and whispers in the dark. Whispers she would never hear.

Tears stung her eyes as he turned and walked away. Oh, God! Since when did she start wearing her heart on her sleeve? When had she become so damned dependent on having him around? TJ sat up straighter and willed her backbone into place.

Tiny was gone. Her role now was to fix the root cause of the problem for once and for all, to keep her promise to Marty and find out who was behind Tiny's death. Ask why Serena Snow was friendly enough with Luke Bennetti's father for him to be chauffeuring her around.

Gino Bennetti was here with his son, Luke and wife, Lily, who appeared to be sporting another shiner. If she was asked about it, she'd say she'd walked into a door, or fell in the garden, but that never explained the fingerprints on her throat or around her wrists. To say Gino Bennetti was an unpleasant man would be putting it mildly. He was a mean bully who would go to untold lengths to win.

TJ's spine cracked with tension as he made his way toward her. Talking to him would be like engaging in verbal warfare. He crossed the floor with all the charm of a bull heading up a stampede, intent on a little trouble making.

'This is the end of your project,' he said as he drew

level with her. 'I'll make sure the mayor pulls the plug on it.'

TJ stood and placed her cup on the table before answering him. 'You can try.'

'I'll do more than try. I'll make it happen. You watch your back, young lady. Nobody likes you or your stupid project.' He stood threateningly close.

'Only because it gets the mules off the street and affects the trade.'

'You're in too deep. You have no idea what you're up against. Back off now. Before someone else gets hurt.'

'Is that a warning?'

'Consider it friendly advice.' His tone sent unpleasant shivers up her spine.

'I'm not good at taking advice. Especially when it comes to the welfare of the kids on the program.'

'Then you really are just a pretty face. Keep your nose out of it and it might stay that way.' The words slipped through his thick lips in a sneer.

'Intimidation is unlawful, Mr Bennetti, as I'm sure you're aware being a lawyer and all yourself. Excuse me, but I have a funeral to wrap up. The funeral of a young boy who was destroyed by the likes of the people you defend. Forgive me if I'm not keen on giving up on saving the rest of them.'

She pushed her way around him, pausing for a split second when he said, 'You've made a very big mistake.'

Her nonchalant shrug was delivered with a confidence she didn't feel as unease churned in her belly. She walked away toward where Scott stood talking to the workshop staff. She stood close to him, closer than she would normally, unsettled by Gino Bennetti's threat.

For the first time since starting the program, she was scared. Tiny's death had been triggered by something bigger than she'd had to deal with before. Her smile was grim as Scott looked down at her, his keen eyes slanting to the slight tremble of her hands. He placed his warm hand over her cold, clasped ones to separate the death grip she had on them that had turned her knuckles white. With a reassuring squeeze, he anchored the hand closest to him to his side. His eyes full of a promise that they would talk about it later.

If there was one good thing that had come out of the tragedy of Tiny's death, it was that Marty had made tentative peace with his mother. She'd attended the funeral and invited Marty home to stay for a couple of days. TJ had agreed to let him go, trying hard not to be afraid that Gino Benetti would go after him. Hopefully, he was too busy plotting against TJ with the Mayor and the judges he had in his back pocket. And Mark had promised a patrol car would do the rounds in the area where Marty's mum lived.

'She told me the little ones miss me,' he said as he threw clothes into his backpack.

'That's a good start. Do you think she wants you to move back for good?' TJ picked up a hoodie out of the ironing basket and shook it out. Folding it neatly, she ran a hand over the comfortably worn polar fleece. The house would be empty without him, even with Scott and Sarge still there.

'Dunno. I treated her pretty badly.' He shrugged. 'Maybe we'll get along better if I don't live with them. Would it be okay if I stayed on with you? I like being here, TJ. Among the trees. Down by the creek. Pottering around. I want to help you finish building the camp.'

Tears stung her eyes. 'I'd be happy for you to stay.'

'Awesome.' He hugged her with the awkwardness of teenage affection; a quick hug of the shoulders before pulling away to bounce on the balls of his feet.

Scott appeared in the doorway of Marty's room. The suit he'd worn to the funeral had been replaced by faded denims and a dark t-shirt that clung to his broad shoulders and caressed his muscled chest.

TJ swallowed past the lump in her throat. How long before he would leave now that Tiny was gone? She tore her eyes from him and looked down to where his dog lay guarding Marty's discarded pile of laundry. They'd all become a part of her life so quickly and easily.

'Ready, champ?' Scott stepped into the room.

'Yeah. Just need to get my toothbrush 'n stuff.' Marty darted out of the room.

'You okay?'

TJ looked up. His eyes searched hers as she nodded tentatively.

'Yep.' The words escaped on a strangled breath.

In a single stride, he had her in his arms with her head resting against the firm pillow of his chest. Raw emotion raged through her as she inhaled his familiar, spicy scent. One strong arm hugged her close as his other hand cupped her head, fingers gently stroking the hair at her temple. Her arms stretched around him, palms flat against the warmth of his back as she burrowed deeper into the comfort of his hold. She felt his lips touch the top of her head as she turned her face into his chest.

'Ready,' said Marty from the doorway.

With a quick hug, Scott gently set her away from him. 'We'll talk when I get back.'

She nodded and squeezed the big, strong hand that lingered on hers before his fingers trailed away down the pulse of her wrist and dropped to his side. Sarge abandoned the laundry to amble across and rub against her legs. She reached down to rub his ears before they followed Scott and Marty out onto the veranda and down the stairs to the car.

TJ and Sarge watched as Bruce carried them down the drive. The cloud of dust they raised drifted up to mingle with the dying rays of the sun as it filtered through the rain clouds and trees. A gentle breeze whispered through the treetops and shivered across her bare arms. Cold crept in through the soles of her bare feet, reminding her that she'd kicked off her shoes as soon as they'd arrived home.

She stood a while longer in the peacefulness of her surroundings, eyes closed as she absorbed the sounds of the running creek, the frantic call of the galahs and the odd laugh of a kookaburra. Beside her, Sarge pressed closer.

'C'mon, Sarge, let's go inside and light the fire.'

The big dog was a comfort as he trailed behind her through the task of closing the house up for the night. TJ lit the fire, closed the curtains and turned on the soft lighting as the sun disappeared from the valley between the hills.

With mechanical movements, she put a casserole in the oven to warm and prepared a bowl of food for Sarge. The evening chill crept along her skin as she placed Sarge's bowl outside the kitchen door to the veranda. Goose flesh reminded her she still wore the sleeveless dress she'd worn to the funeral. Leaving the door ajar so Sarge could wander in when he was done, she turned to walk back through the lounge to her room.

A pile of mail lay forgotten on the coffee table. When had Scott brought it in? Since he and Tiny had moved in, he'd gotten into the habit of picking it up from the post office box on his way home from work. Days had melded into one another since Tiny's disappearance. Mail was a reminder of the need to return to normality. TJ picked up the envelopes and flicked through the advertising to find the bills. Her hand stilled on a white envelope addressed to her in the spidery, immature handwriting she recognized as Tiny's.

Her heart pounded as she checked the date stamp. It had been mailed the day after he'd disappeared. She ripped the envelope open and took out the crumpled piece of lined paper torn from an exercise book. Hands shaking, she unfolded it and read:

TJ, if u r reading this the writing is on the wall. Tell Scott I didn't bail. I wanted to stay and make good, but they came after me. I asked Connor to mail this if anything happened. I can't trust anyone else. Marty and Connor will be safe. I'm worried about Luke. There's more. The writing is on the wall. Terence B Watts

Icy fingers crawled up TJ's spine. What did he mean? Something hovered at the edge of her conscience, but her mind was too tired and emotionally drained to capture it. Sarge pushed in through the back door and she walked into the kitchen to close it behind him. No point letting the heat of the fire out. As she dropped the roman blind down over the window, she thought she saw a flicker of light down at the end of her driveway. She looked again but it was dark, and nothing moved. A passing car making a turn? It didn't matter.

Scott would be home soon. The letter had made her antsy.

'Come, Sarge.'

Sarge fell into step behind her as she walked up the corridor to her room. As she passed the closed door to Tiny's room, a shiver of unease ran up her spine again. Why had Tiny signed his real name on the letter? Even on his apprenticeship application he'd signed it as 'Tiny'. She retraced her steps and placed her hand on the cold brass door knob. Sarge whined.

'It's okay, boy. Stay close.'

She took a deep breath before turning the knob and pushing the door open. No one had been in the room since Forensics had searched it for clues when Tiny had disappeared and again when his body had been found. Fingerprint dust still marked the edges of his chest of drawers.

TJ picked her way over the scattered electronics, earphones, laptop and discarded laundry that littered the floor. She tossed a crumpled pile of shirts onto the unmade bed. It was exactly as he'd left it, except for the odd pieces the detectives had taken as evidence.

What did he mean about the writing being on the wall? She looked around the dim room. There was no graffiti on the walls. Sarge sniffed around under the bed before moving across to the chest of drawers. He stood on his hind legs against it and sniffed at the jumble of things that lay on top. Distracted, TJ walked over to rub his ears and he dropped down to sit at her feet. Her eyes fell on the clutter. A couple of pens, an earring, a box of matches, his watch and a braided leather bracelet lay on top of a notebook.

She snapped on the wax lamp that stood next to the collection. Its orange glow picked out a picture on the cover of the notebook. Tiny had graffitied the front of the notebook. Not just random scribbling, but a colourful mural with so much detail, you'd need to study it for a while to read it all. She'd had no idea Tiny was this creative. *Terence B Watts* sprawled across three coloured bricks in fat green writing.

TJ sat down on the floor with her back against the bed clutching the notebook to her chest. A lump formed in her throat and tears stung her eyes, increasing to spill over onto her cheeks as Sarge flopped down beside and put his head on her lap. She lay down beside him and cried into his fur until she fell asleep, exhausted.

The house was in darkness as Scott pulled up. Where was TJ? Had she gone over to Mum's? He glanced at the illuminated clock on the dash. No, it was too late. And Sarge? Normally he came bounding down the stairs at the sound of a car. Unease gripped his stomach. He manoeuvred his long legs from out behind the wheel, got out and shut the door. Still nothing moved in the house. Maybe she'd fallen asleep before switching on the lights. The automatic sensor light switched on to illuminate the front door as he opened it and went inside. He really needed to remind her to lock it.

'TJ?' The smell of the warming casserole made his stomach growl as he walked into the kitchen. The oven light glowed dimly in the dark room, showing the casserole bubbling away. He snapped on the light and turned off the oven. As he walked up the corridor, he heard Sarge whine and followed the sound. The door to Tiny's room stood open. As he stepped through it he saw TJ asleep on the carpet with her arm slung around Sarge's body and her head resting on him like a fur pillow.

He smiled. Her hair had come loose and spread over Sarge like a blanket. One hand clutched his fur, the other hugged a book to her stomach. In the well created by her curled body and drawn up knees, lay a scribbled note.

Sarge met his look with a sad, resigned one of his own as he yawned in greeting. Scott bent to scratch his ears.

'I'll move her in a minute,' he said, and Sarge lay his big brown head back on his paws with a sigh.

Asleep, TJ reminded him of a sleeping tiger with all the cuddly innocence of a kitten. Awake, she was fearless, ferocious and untameable. And he loved her.

He'd expected that knowledge to slam into him. Instead, it had grown around him over the last few months as he'd watched her throw everything she had into her work, into the project and into creating a stable home life for lost boys not much younger than herself. Then he'd watched her go to pieces when she lost one while trying to keep it together for those who remained.

Yes, he loved her. He wanted to stay here in this little piece of paradise and grow old with her by his side. He wanted to be there when she filled the finished cabins with more lost children and made a difference, even a small one, to society.

Scott knelt on the carpet and brushed the hair from her cheeks. She mumbled, pushed her face into Sarge's fur and stretched her legs out. The movement made the skirt of her black dress ride up her thigh. For God's sake, did she think he was made of stone?

His eyes followed the length of her firm, shapely legs down past the slim ankles to her delicate feet.

'C'mon, Sleeping Beauty. Time for bed.' He shook her shoulder gently.

TJ lifted her head and muttered before laying it back down on the dog's warm body. Scott grinned. 'Okay, you've forced my hand. Now I'll have to carry you to bed.'

A slow, dreamy smile spread across her lips. 'Mmm,' she purred and curled up again.

Scott took several deep breaths and reminded himself that he was a gentleman who didn't ravish sleeping princesses. He looped her arm around his neck and slid one arm under her shoulders and the other in the crook of her legs to hoist her into his arms.

'Book,' she mumbled against his chest where he'd taken off his tie and loosened a few buttons.

The graze of her lips against his skin sent white heat searing through him. 'I'll get it later.'

Her free arm came up to join the other one around his neck as she sank against him. 'Warm.' She pressed her face into his neck.

Scott's arms tightened. At this rate, he'd need more than a cold shower. He pushed open her door with his foot and laid her down on the bed before prying her arms from around his neck. She mumbled and shook her head.

'You can't sleep in that dress, love. You need to take it off. Where's your PJs?'

She protested as he tugged at the skirt. 'No.'

'It's going to be uncomfortable and itchy in the morning,' he warned.

She turned over on her stomach and exposed the zipper. 'Off,' she mumbled.

'That's not a good idea, Tiger.'

He dug around under her pillow and came up with a T-shirt which he shoved into her hand and closed her fingers around. 'Put that on, TJ.' The skirt had ridden almost to her waist exposing a very neat, tight bottom in a pair of lacy black, barely-there knickers. Scott groaned and promised himself a long, cold shower and something stronger than coffee. He tickled the soles of her feet. 'Wake up. When I come back I want you out of that dress and under the covers.'

She stretched like a cat and the skirt hiked higher. Scott closed his eyes and mentally doubled the dash of whiskey he'd put in his glass tonight.

'S' that an invitation?' Her sleepy voice stopped him in his tracks.

He walked to the en suite and gripped the door frame to stop himself from turning around. 'Not tonight.'

Silence stretched and he thought she'd gone back to sleep until she said, 'Scott?'

'Yeah?'

'Thanks.'

'Okay. Get into your PJs now. I'll check on you after I've had my shower.'

'Scott?'

He bit his lip and prayed for the strength of a gentleman. 'Yes?'

'Can you undo my zipper?'

Sarge echoed his groan from the floor at the foot of the bed.

'You might have to take care of that yourself, sweetheart. Much safer for both of us.' He closed the bathroom door with a little more force than necessary.

Chapter Sixteen

The gentle hiss of the shower and the groan of the pipes drew TJ out of her half slumber. With a sigh, she raised herself up off her stomach and rolled off the bed. Her hands searched for Tiny's book. Unease crawled in the pit of her stomach. Sarge lifted his head with a short sharp bark. She leaned down to rub his head.

'Yes, I know he's home.' The comforting noises from the bathroom held the familiar sounds of Scott's movements. 'Stay here.'

TJ padded out the door and down the corridor to Tiny's room where she picked the book up off the floor. A flicker of orange light reflected off the window. In the silence, the crackle and pop of burning wood reached her ears at the same time as the smell of smoke curled toward her nose.

Odd. Had Scott stoked the wood fire? A check of the lounge room showed the wood fire had damped down to glowing coals. The same orange glow bounced around the room. Bushfire… With one hand on her mobile phone, she rushed over to the window and swept the curtains aside. Up the hill, the partially renovated cabins glowed orange as flames crept up the walls.

TJ swore as she dialled the emergency number for the fire department. Icy terror surged down her spine. A bushfire here would race through the hills and destroy everything in its path. Only a few months earlier, the spark from a grinder had set the bush alight and the wind had driven the blaze across the hills taking houses and the bridge with it. TJ's stomach churned.

Barefoot, she raced out the door and to the shed, shouting the address into the phone as she went. Woodchips and gravel dug into her feet as she wedged the phone between her cheek and shoulder and struggled with the lock. Tossing the phone on the ground, she wrenched the heavy door open on its sliders and hit the start button on the pump that sent water from the wells into the sprinklers around the property.

Sparks ignited the surrounding grass as the fire took hold. She turned open the tap on the garden hose to full and ran toward the fire with it. The hose unravelled from its coil like a snake, spitting and hissing as water spurted in sharp bursts with increasing pressure. TJ aimed the hose at the grass in front of her, dampening the ground ahead of the fire. There was no time to think or feel as she battled against the growing flames.

'Jesus!' Scott's shout from behind had her turning around.

'I've called the FES. Call your dad and tell him to spread the word to the neighbours.' She coughed as smoke stung her lungs. 'I need you to clear a firebreak where it's heading up the back fence. Equipment's in the shed.'

Scott pulled off his cotton shirt and wet it in the stream of water from the hose. He squeezed the excess water out before wrapping it around her neck and covering her mouth. With a quick hug, he sprinted to the shed as he dialled his father's number. Fifteen minutes later, he was clearing the firebreak while TJ dampened the ground around it when the Fire and Emergency Services arrived.

The shouts of the fire-fighters blended with the hiss and spit of the water as it sizzled over the flames. Still the fire licked at the blackening walls of the cabins, driven by an unseen accelerant. She stepped back to give the fire-fighters access, oblivious of the pain in the soles of her feet where loose stones and bush debris had pierced the skin. Her eyes burned with the heat of the fire and tears she refused to let fall.

Hopes, dreams, all destroyed in a single heartbeat.

Who would do this? Who would be so vengeful as to risk an entire community to destroy a refuge? All those months of hard work, petitions, cutting through red tape, battles with the council and back-breaking renovation … all gone.

Exhaustion hovered as she swayed, and her vision blurred. Months of pent-up emotions swelled to the surface. Screw being brave, she was tired, so tired of the struggle to keep the dream alive. The pressure on her chest was almost unbearable as she swallowed back the pain squeezing at her heart.

First Tiny … now the cabins. At least Marty wasn't there to see the devastation. She flinched as a gentle hand touched her ash-covered arm.

'Come, love,' Rose's soft voice reached her ears. 'There's nothing more you can do here. The boys will have it under control in no time.'

The garden hose had gone slack in her hand. She stared at it unseeingly, as someone unravelled the now dry, crisp shirt from her face and neck. A warm, comforting arm settled around her shoulders as a hand removed the hose from her numbed fingers. Another encouraging hand on the small of her back gently urged her to turn around and walk toward the house, but her feet remained frozen.

'Scott,' called Rose, her voice urgent as TJ sank to her knees on the warm, blackened ground.

Strong hands slipped under her arms and drew her to her feet. Numb, she turned around unseeingly and buried her face in the comfort of his chest. His arms encircled her as he drew her closer for a moment.

'C'mon, let's get you cleaned up,' he said against her smoky hair.

The thud of the fire engine's water pump matched the dull thud in her head, beat for beat, as she lifted her face and pushed away. Needles of pain shot up through her feet as she stepped back and she winced.

'Ah, Tiger, where are your shoes?'

Before she could protest, she was in his arms and cradled against him. Too tired to argue, she let her pounding head drop against his shoulder and clung to his grimy undershirt.

'You get her cleaned up while I make a pot of tea,' said Rose as she led the way up to the house.

Scott hoisted TJ closer as he negotiated his way through the door. For a moment, he hesitated. It might be better if he made the tea and left the cleaning up to his mother but as TJ sighed in his arms, he knew he couldn't let that happen.

'Thanks, Mum.' His wry grin spoke volumes as he made his way up the corridor, through the bedroom and into the bathroom. 'Sit here for a minute while I find us some clean clothes.'

He lowered her to sit on the closed toilet seat and

she leaned her head back on the cool, porcelain cistern. Minutes later he was back, turning on taps and adjusting the water temperature. TJ stood unsteadily to her feet and reached behind her back for the zipper of her dress. Her tired muscles protested, and she dropped her arms to her side.

'Can you get my zipper?' She swayed with fatigue as she turned and presented her back to him.

He gripped her shoulders to steady her before inching the zipper down and sliding the dress off her shoulders. 'Will you be okay in the shower on your own?'

She hesitated before shaking her head. 'Stay with me.'

'That's a big ask.'

'I know.'

'It could change the rules.'

'Yes.'

'Are you sure you want to do that?'

'Yes. We're wasting water.' Still with her back to him, she stepped out of the lacy boy-legs and tossed them in the laundry basket.

Scott sighed as his appreciative glance swept up those shapely legs to find them attached to an equally shapely and firm round bottom. As he reached for the fly of his jeans, the matching bra followed the path of the boy legs, and he was awarded a glimpse of what she kept secret under her crazy T-shirts – like the one that said *my eyes are up here*.

'Last chance to change your mind.'

She stepped into the flow of warm water and lifted her face to let it sluice down her body. 'Why waste more water? I'm too damn tired to take advantage of you.'

'That's what I'm afraid of.' He whipped off his remaining clothes and stepped in behind her.

She leaned back against his warm chest with a sigh. 'Thank you.'

He reached around her for the soap and held it in front of her face. 'You're torturing me here. My mum is in the kitchen making tea.'

TJ smiled and took the soap from him. He reached around her again for the shampoo. The slide of her silky skin against his sent his blood rushing and he dropped a kiss on her smooth shoulder. She tipped her head back to expose the length of her neck and sighed with pleasure. His lips followed the line up along her jaw to the corner of her mouth.

'A cup of tea sounds nice.' She turned her mouth to meet his.

He nibbled her lower lip. 'This is nicer.' It took all his strength not to run his hands down her curves and turn her into him. 'But at any moment now, Mum will be knocking on the door and I'm sure the fire chief will have some questions for us.'

She sighed heavily and turned around, her breasts

brushing against his him. He sucked in his breath as her arms came around him to soap his back. For a torturous moment he let her have her way as he dispensed the shampoo and massaged it through her hair. Wet, it fell like a silk curtain to rest in the small of her back.

'Rinse,' he ordered hoarsely.

She leaned back under the spray as her hands slipped down to grip his rear for balance. The muscles rippled in response to the clutch of her fingers. His hands ran the length of her back as her lower body angled closer to his. He took a moment to admire the rosy, pink buds that tipped her firm, round breasts and willed his body to behave. Too late. He drew her back up against him and reached behind her to turn off the taps.

'We'll finish this later.'

'Yes,' she whispered against his chest.

Seconds later, a warm, fluffy towel descended around her shoulders as he stepped away from her lips and out of the cubicle.

'Let's get the preliminaries out the way. The sooner we call it a night, the better.' And with a little bit of luck, she would be asleep on her feet and the temptation of her lips would be removed.

TJ stepped out of the cubicle and winced as her feet touched the cold tiles. Scott looked down and saw the nicks and cuts caused by loose bark and twigs as she'd danced with the hose to dampen the ground around the fire. With a sigh, he wrapped her in the towel, swept her into his arms, whisked her through the doorway and dropped her gently in the middle of her bed.

'Stay there,' he ordered, tugging on his shorts and heading for the door.

Minutes later he returned with a mug of tea in one hand and a bottle of aloe vera gel, cold from the fridge, in the other. 'I sent Mum home to get some sleep.'

He wasn't sure whether to be pleased or disappointed that she'd tugged on fresh boy-legs and a singlet. Propped up against the pillows, she looked pale and tired. He handed her the mug of tea, which she grasped with both hands, embracing the warmth.

'Thanks.' She sighed with pleasure, and he watched her throat work to swallow another sip of the warm liquid. She closed her eyes and rested her head back against the pillows.

With a snap of the lid, Scott up ended the bottle of aloe vera with an impatient shake and dispensed a dollop of the cool liquid onto his finger. The mattress dipped under his weight as he sat facing her, his thigh warm against her calf.

He recited the semi-final footy scores in his head as he stroked the sticky gel down a scratch on her velvety cheek with his forefinger and smoothed it with his thumb. He forgot the words to the West Coast Eagles club song and had to start again when she pressed her cheek into the palm of his hand and dropped a kiss on the pad at the base of his thumb.

It was hard to ignore the fire that spread through his belly from that simple action. He dropped his hand to rest next to her knees, reddened by the heat of the fire and chafe of the garden hose against them as she'd moved.

'Mark Johnson will be back tomorrow with the fire chief to ask us a few questions. There's not much more they can do tonight. The fire is almost out. They'll be back in the daylight to search for the source.' He smoothed more gel on her reddened legs as she nodded tiredly.

'Thanks.'

He lifted her foot, and she bent her knee to rest it on his upper thigh. For a moment, he studied the delicate, pink-tipped toes usually hidden by steel caps and traced the arch of her instep with his thumb. Her toes curled into the crease at the top of his thigh. Her eyelids fluttered as she felt his body respond and her cheeks glowed pink.

She tried to shift her foot out of his grasp, but his grip tightened as he tipped it up and massaged the cool liquid into her sole.

'Scott?' she croaked, as he treated the other foot to the same attention.

His throat tightened around the words as they rose to his lips. 'Don't. Say. A. Word,' he snapped through clenched teeth and smoothed gel around the underside of her ankle bone.

She whimpered a little as he stroked the sensitive flesh behind her knee where a sharp-edged branch had left a raised welt, squeezed her knuckles against her lips when the flat of his palm reached the top of her thigh. The empty mug slipped from her fingers.

Wordlessly, Scott swept it up and knelt to lean up over her and set it down on the table beside the bed. His stomach clenched as her fingers fluttered across his skin, up over the light dusting of hair on his chest and up further to cup his cheek. Her thumb feathered over his lips.

'Thank you,' she whispered as her hand moved to cup his neck and draw him closer.

'You're welcome,' he whispered against her mouth.

Her lips moved against his, teasing, testing, tasting until he lowered himself to place his elbows on either side of her tantalizing body. Dragging his lips from hers, he cupped her face.

'Now would be a good time for me to go back to my own room.'

Panic flared in her eyes. 'No! Please stay.'

'I'm not sure that's a good idea.'

'For the first time in my life, I'm scared. Please stay with me tonight? First Tiny, now the fire…'

Scott pressed a finger to her lips. 'I know, love, but if I stay we're going to be breaking a few rules.'

'Maybe life is too short for rules,' she said and nipped the pad of his finger.

'Maybe … but you'll see things differently in the morning.' He drew in a shaky breath as her hand covered his and she pried his fingers loose to plant a chain of kisses from his palm to his wrist. 'What if…'

His words disappeared into flesh as she covered his mouth with her free hand.

'No what-ifs tonight. I have nothing else left. All I have right now is tonight.'

'We still have Marty, Connor and Luke. We can rebuild.'

She shook her head against the pillow. The drying strands of her hair spread across it and glistened reddish gold in the soft lamplight as she moved. 'No, it's over. I can't keep rebuilding.' Tears slipped down her cheeks.

Scott trailed kisses against the salty curve of her eyes. 'We'll rebuild together.'

When her fingers caressed his hair and moved to forge a fiery trail down his back, Scott knew he couldn't resist her. As her arms edged him closer, he admitted he was lost and happy to remain that way. With every touch and slide of her silky skin against his, it felt like coming home. And when he finally slipped inside her, he knew for sure he'd found love.

~

TJ eased out from under Scott's heavy arm. For a brief moment, she watched him sleep. The bone-deep weariness that had threatened to overtake her had fled in the wake of his kisses last night. With each touch and whisper, she'd felt invigorated, alive and, for the first time in months, perhaps even years, she'd fallen into a peaceful sleep, wrapped in the strength and comfort of his arms.

Now, in the cold, hard light of day, reality struck hard. She slipped into track pants and a hoodie and padded across the carpeted room in bare feet to the door. Scott's careful attention to her feet had eased the scratch and burn of her injuries. Injuries that were now a reminder of what they'd lost.

Sarge gave up his post at the bedroom door and trailed behind her into the kitchen. TJ unlocked the back door and opened it to let him out for his morning sniff-and-scratch. Through the misty haze that hung low across the valley, the shadowy shape of the ruined cottages loomed, cordoned off with reflective yellow and red caution tape.

Wisps of smoke mingled with the mist as the piles of burnt wood and board still smouldered in the cool morning air. As Sarge trailed back in and passed her, she closed the door on the ghostly reminder of their dream reduced to rubble.

When had she started to think of it as theirs not hers? It was hard to remember how life had been before

Scott Devin had entered her world and taken some of the load off her shoulders.

And last night … TJ leaned her back against the door and closed her eyes. God, what a night! They'd moved in unison, like dance partners who'd spent a lifetime anticipating each other's choreographed moves.

She wanted to believe it was a one-off. Comfort sex, nothing more. But there was no point kidding herself. Last night they'd formed a bond that went beyond anything she'd experienced before. Nothing would ever be the same again.

The kettle boiled and clicked off. TJ poured the boiling water into the cups and stirred to mix in the coffee granules. The rich, roasted, familiar aroma was absurdly comforting, as was the mundaneness of the task. Behind her, Scott padded into the kitchen. His morning sock shuffle was now as familiar as the landscape that surrounded them. She could tell his steps apart from Marty and Tiny's.

Tiny. Surely there were no more tears left to cry? Yet as Scott's arms slipped around her and pulled her into the warmth of his chest, a few escaped down her cheeks. She dashed them away and stroked the arms that enveloped her. With a sigh, she rested her head against his chest and accepted the kiss he pressed to her temple.

'Coffee's ready,' she said as he gently set her away from him to scratch Sarge's ears.

'Thanks.' He reached around her for his mug with a

quick one-armed hug. 'Have you had a look outside yet?'

'The mist is still a little heavy. They've taped off the area.' She turned to snuggle into him. As his free hand drew circles in the curve of her back, she purred a little.

His chest vibrated with a chuckle against her ear and mingled with his slightly unsteady heartbeat. 'Any more of that, Tiger and you won't be available to watch that mist burn off.'

Reality coldly intruded and she lifted her head. 'I'm not sure I want to see what's left.'

'With a bit of luck, the structural walls will be okay. Those clay bricks the Brickworks donated are fairly resistant.'

TJ stiffened. 'The writing is on the wall…'

'What?'

She pushed at his chest, and he stepped back. 'Tiny's book! Where is it?'

'What book?'

Excitement speared through her belly. 'Last night I found a note from Tiny. And a notebook with drawings on the cover. I had it with me in his room. No … the fire. In the lounge room …' Her coffee mug hit the bench top with a thud and splashed liquid down the cupboard doors, which Sarge happily licked clean as she disappeared through the doorway. Within seconds she was back, clutching a notebook in one hand and a ragged piece of paper in the other.

Scott pushed away from the bench to peer over her shoulder. 'I didn't realize Tiny could draw so well.'

'Neither did I. In his note he said something about the writing being on the wall.' Chair legs scraped across the jarrah floor as they sat down at the kitchen table. TJ placed the notebook and the letter between them on its surface.

Scott pulled the notebook toward him and studied the artwork on the cover. 'This is very detailed. It must have taken him ages to do.' Long fingers stroked the cover before well-groomed nails tapped out a tattoo against the wooden surface of the table.

For a fleeting moment, TJ was distracted by the rhythm. Those same fingers had stroked her back last night until she'd drifted into a comfortable sleep against his chest. She watched as those magic fingers picked up the crumpled note.

'Tiny never used his birth name. Why would he graffiti it onto his course notebook?'

'Good question,' Scott murmured. He smoothed the note out against the cover of the book. 'And he signed the note with his full name too.'

'A clue?'

'Maybe.' He moved his chair around the table to sit next to her. 'Look at this.' His forefinger drew a line under the fat green letters. 'The 'N' and the 'E' in 'Terence' are capitals. Further down 'Watts' is crossed out and replaced by 'wall'. Could he be referring to a north-east wall? But the wall of what? The clubhouse?'

Excitement mingled with fear in the pit of TJ's stomach. 'No, it can't be. The clubhouse was removed by the police after Marty OD'd. His bedroom faces north-east, but I checked the walls in there last night. Nothing there.'

Scott's hand came to rest on her knee with a little squeeze and she rested her head against his extended arm for a moment.

'Look at these snakes he's drawn on the bottom. It looks like they're crawling along the concrete.'

'They form shapes …'

'No, initials.' Scott lifted the book closer to study the drawings. 'S S and C? Looks like an inverted E.'

'No, I think it's a G. Look, the snake curls with its head facing up the wall. The tongue is forked but the forks stretch to left and right rather than upward. The 'E' is a 'B'. It lines up with the edge of the brick.'

'Clever girl, good spotting.'

'SS and GB?' Unease crept along her spine. She shivered.

Scott set the notebook down on the table and scooted his chair back. 'We'll have to give these to Mark when they come around later to investigate the fire.'

'Yes, I suppose we do. What do you suppose he meant about Luke?'

Scott shrugged and tugged her closer. 'Don't know. How well do you know Luke?'

TJ didn't resist his pull and straddled his lap, hooking her legs around the narrow backrest. 'Tiny, Marty, Connor and Luke have been friends since primary school.' Firm hands cupped her bottom and pulled her closer. She clasped her hands behind his head. 'They formed the gang when they got to high school. From what Marty's told me, it was a preservation thing against bullying during recess.'

Scott wriggled down a little in the chair and grinned at the sigh of pleasure that escaped her lips as their lower bodies aligned. 'Perfect match. Where did it start to go wrong?'

She leaned forward to drop a kiss on his parted lips, her breasts brushing tantalizingly against his chest as she did so. It was his turn to sigh as she rested her forehead against his neck.

'Luke got into drugs first. He was always the dark horse. An unhappy kid, almost unreachable at times. Gino Bennetti, Luke's father, might be a lawyer but he's as crooked as they come. Both mother and son have ended up sporting suspicious injuries. You saw Lily's black eye.'

Silence weighed heavily between them at the reality of Lily and Luke's situation.

'Bastard,' Scott muttered. 'So, with Luke hooked, it didn't take long for the others to fall?'

'Sadly, no. The good thing is they all still stuck together. The only one that doesn't seem to fit the profile is Connor.'

'How?'

With a sigh, she moved off his lap and walked over to the kitchen window with its view up the hill of the cabins. 'Unlike the others, Connor comes from a stable home. His parents are well off, were happily married as far as anyone was aware and both care deeply for him. Until recently, they were a well-rounded, perfect happy family.'

'Maybe a little too perfect? What happened?'

TJ shrugged. 'No one really knows much, but Connor's dad left them a little over a month ago.'

Silently, she watched as the sun pierced through the veil of mist and it began to skitter away. *The sun rises in the east and sets in the west.* The words tumbled through her mind as she looked north, skimming over the remains of an old brick fireplace and chimney, the only part of one of the original 1940s cabins left standing.

Her body froze for an instant. 'That's it!' she yelled, moving away from the window to yank open the back door.

'What?' Scott's chair crashed over as he leapt up to bound after her.

'The wall!' Her voice bounced in time to the pounding of her feet on the ground.

'Jesus, woman! I wish you'd remember to put your shoes on before you take off. What wall?'

She stopped suddenly and he almost fell over her. His hands reached for her arms, more to steady himself than her. She cupped his face between her hands and planted an excited kiss on his lips.

'The chimney wall … It faces north-east. Tiny could see it from his bedroom window which also faces north-east.'

'That's a long shot.'

'It's the only shot we have!' She walked more slowly toward the crumbling chimney. 'What did chimneys have?'

Scott shook his head. 'I have no idea. You tell me.'

'During the war, this area was used for transmitting radio signals because of its high points.' Excitement boiled to the surface as she spoke. 'The houses were built with hidey holes in which secret or sensitive messages could be stored and not found by the enemy. One of the least popular but not unusual places to hide things was in the chimney.' She stopped and peered inside the empty cavern of the old fire pit. 'Who was small enough to fit inside there?' Her head tipped toward the rear where the wall was blackened by decades of soot and a fresh layer added from the night before.

'Tiny,' said Scott as he too peered into the chimney.

'But he said the writing was on the wall, not in the wall.'

TJ sat on the floor and scooted backwards into the deep cavern. 'They built these deep back then to avoid sparks from the fireplace escaping and setting the house alight.' She peered up into the darkness of the chimney and reached above her head. Her fingers explored the dark recesses of the chimney stack.

'Should you be doing that? Aren't there Redback spiders in there?'

'If there are and I get bitten, it will be worth the pain and suffering. Just make sure you get me the antivenin as quickly as possible.'

The bite of the Redback spider would leave her stiff, sore and very ill. With a little bit of luck, the smoke and heat from last night's fire would have sent them off to new breeding places, hopefully taking any babies with them. Black soot dislodged from the walls and dusted her hair and face. She sneezed and wiped her face with her sleeve, leaving a streak across her cheek.

'Got it!'

Scott found himself smiling as her teeth gleamed white in her soot-blackened face. 'What have you got?'

'A loose brick.' It landed at his feet. 'And…' A roll of paper wrapped in plastic appeared in her extended fist. Scott took it gingerly from her as she scooted out of the fireplace on her bottom. He extended a hand to help but she shook her head. 'One of us covered in grime is enough.'

Scott tapped the plastic covered paper against the seat of his shorts to dislodge some of the soot with a wicked gleam in his eyes. 'I'm not averse to sharing another shower.' His arms encircled her to hold her loosely.

TJ reached out and ran a grimy finger down his bare chest, leaving a trail of soot in its wake. 'Maybe after we see what legacy Tiny has left behind.'

Chapter Seventeen

'TJ? Scott? Are you home?' Rob's voice rang out from the house.

'Out the back, Rob!' TJ pulled out of Scott's arms. With a grin, she planted a kiss on his chest. 'If you hurry inside my brother won't have the opportunity to rag you about your … well, you know.'

His chest rumbled against her lips. 'I can handle the ribbing, but I'll save you the embarrassment.'

Firm lips brushed against the top of her head before she watched him walk away. TJ took a moment to admire the cling of the cotton as it caressed the sway of his hips and buttocks. With a sigh she turned toward the house to head her brother off so Scott could slip inside.

'Hey, Rob,' she greeted as she reached the front veranda.

He stood, hands on hips, mouth drawn tight as his

sweeping gaze took stock of the damage. 'Fuck! What happened?'

'We had a little trouble last night.'

'No shit!'

'Ah, Robert, I can always rely on you to sum things up for me.' She grinned and reached up to kiss his cheek.

He nudged her off. 'Hey, white shirt here. Want to tell me why you look like you've been playing in the chimney?'

'Because I have. Looking for clues.'

'Isn't that a job for the Fire Inspector?'

'Not those sorts of clues, these sorts of clues …' She whipped the plastic-wrapped roll of paper out of her hoodie pocket and whacked him on the chest with it.

'You've lost me.'

'That's okay, you'll catch up.'

'Where's Scott?'

Her eyes flickered away, and she couldn't stop the mischievous grin that curved her lips. 'He'll be out in a moment. Hopefully with coffee.'

Rob's eyes narrowed on her face as he caught the raise in her voice on the tail end of her sentence. 'Something you want to tell me?'

'Ah … nope.' She poked him in the ribs. 'Mind your own business, big brother.'

Rob shrugged. 'No harm in asking. Now, what's in

the plastic?' His forefinger flicked against the roll in her hand.

'We were just about to find out. Come on over and take a seat on the veranda while I go inside and get the rest of the puzzle.'

Rob strolled over to where the chairs overlooked the creek. Sarge had taken up his usual position next to TJ's favourite chair and sat to attention with a short bark. He sniffed at Rob's outstretched hand and, when satisfied he posed no threat, lay back down with a watchful eye.

'Maybe you should wash off some of that war paint before you take those papers out of the wrapper.' Rob pressed a forefinger to the sooty smudge she'd left behind after poking his ribs.

'Good point. Give me five minutes. I'll send Scott out to keep you company.'

'I'm not sure it's my company Scott's interested in.'

'You're a riot, Robert.' She slammed the screen door on his wicked chuckle.

Ten minutes later, TJ stepped back out onto the veranda. Scott glanced up from where Tiny's notebook lay between him and Rob on the table. He took a long moment to admire the jeans that clung lovingly to her slim legs and rode gently on her hips. His gaze licked over the skin bared between the waistband and the hem of her t-shirt. *Is your motor running hot,* the slogan asked, with a red check-engine symbol beneath it. He pulled a chair closer to him and patted the seat.

Her leg grazed against his as she sat. Heat surged through him as he draped an arm on the backrest behind her shoulders and pressed a mug of coffee into her grasp with his free hand.

'Thank you.' Her eyes rose to his and a smile softened her lips.

'You're welcome,' he murmured against her temple as his thumb stroked her shoulder.

'Are we going to solve this mystery, or do you two need some time alone?'

'Cute, Robert. Hand me the papers we found in the chimney stack.' TJ put her coffee down and held out her hand for the plastic-wrapped parcel. She stripped the layers of cling film off and spread the lined notebook paper out on the table. The edges curled over Tiny's spidery handwriting.

'Looks like a list,' said Scott, scooting closer. His arm dropped from around her shoulders, and he placed his hand on her upper thigh. Heat coiled as he traced a line down to her knee.

'It is. Names, places, dates … Look, Paul Price is listed here. Isn't he the guy who was arrested in Williams for kidnapping his stepdaughter?' TJ lowered the mug from her lips and gripped Scott's wandering hand as it trailed back up her thigh.

'That and money laundering,' said Rob as he picked up the notebook and studied the graffiti art. 'He was defended by Gino Bennetti. What a coincidence.' Sarcasm dripped from Rob's tone. The finger that traced the snakes on the artwork stilled. 'GB – Gino Bennetti? But who is SS and why are they in Tiny's drawing?'

'Gino is Luke's father. Is it a coincidence that he owns a car like the one Tiny was last seen in?' Her easy smile turned grim as her gaze searched his face. 'And what was Serena Snow doing in his car when she paid you a visit, Scott?'

Scott continued to scan the list wordlessly. The hand that had caressed her leg was still now, fingers tense. Scott pulled his hand away and fisted it on the top of his thigh. His stomach plummeted. His eyes read the data even as his mind refused to accept facts. He forced a shuttered look to clear his face of expression. The walls slammed back into place.

'SS,' murmured Rob. 'Serena Snow.'

'We need to hand these over to the police. Now.'

TJ's voice seemed to come from a distance as red-hot anger blurred Scott's vision. The date and address on the page might as well have been written in neon. If the list became evidence, he'd be an accessory to murder.

'And here they are now,' said Rob, as Detective Mark Johnson steered his unmarked car up the steep incline to the house.

They stood and turned to the approaching car. TJ

stepped closer to Scott, seeking the comfort of his warmth. Instead, she met with cold, solid rock. Confusion warred with uncertainty in her expression, but he refused to meet her eyes. He stared ahead, his jaw set as Detective Johnson and his partner Harold Jones approached the veranda.

'Mark, Harold.' TJ set her shoulders and stepped forward to greet them.

'Hey, TJ.' Mark placed a hand on her shoulder and squeezed tightly before nodding to the two men who stood behind her.

'Will Forensics be up soon to look for evidence?' she asked.

'They're right behind us.' He waved a hand toward the driveway where a white four-wheel drive branded with the blue police forensics unit logo had stopped at the edge of the burnt-out bushland. The lines around Mark's mouth tightened. 'But we're here on another matter which may be related to your recent troubles.' His expression hardened further as he looked past her at Scott. 'Mr Devin, we need you to come down to the station with us for questioning.'

'What?' TJ choked on the word. 'Scott?' She turned to him, her eyes searching, her hands reaching for him.

Scott ignored her outstretched hands, stepping around her instead. Muscles corded in his neck as he swallowed around the lump in his throat. Silently he handed Mark the list scribbled on a page from Tiny's notebook. 'You'll need this. And the notebook.'

'Scott? Mark?'

The terror that laced TJ's voice almost had him turning around and wrapping her in his arms. Instead, he let Harold Jones take his arm and lead him away to the car.

'I'm sorry, TJ. I can't explain right now. All I can tell you is that we received a tip off. What's the go with the notebook?'

Numb, TJ stared after Scott as Rob handed over the notebook.

'Tiny left a letter for TJ and clues in the graffiti on the book. Through it we found that list hidden in the ruined fire place. You'll need to get someone to study that picture really carefully. Tiny was a lot smarter than he let on.'

'I'll get someone onto it. In the meanwhile, TJ please stay away from the site of the fire. We can't have evidence being compromised now. This wasn't an accident. The heat and rate at which the fire spread suggests that whoever started it used an accelerant. We won't know more until the results of the investigation are in.'

With a fist jammed to her mouth, she nodded.

'I'll call you as soon as we have something.'

Evening shadows stretched out to touch the corners of the empty house; the only light came from the flickering images on the television screen. The hum of the six o'clock news filled the silence. TJ stared unseeingly at the screen and wondered if she would ever feel anything but numb again.

Rose and Bill were in lockdown against the television crews that swarmed the hill waiting to pounce on a comment. The police had managed to keep them off the property while they finished their investigation into the fire. Now it was dark, maybe they'd go away. Tomorrow they would be back, hounds on the scent of a juicy bone.

Next to her, Sarge's soft snores provided little comfort. She hugged the cushion closer to her chest. The television flickered back to the studio where the newsreader stared grim-faced into the camera.

'Breaking news tonight from the Perth hills where well-known local businessman Scott Devin has been detained for questioning in regard to the death of Terence Watts. New evidence has come to light which implicates Mr Devin in the disappearance and subsequent death of the eighteen-year-old. Terence was an apprentice under the controversial teenage rehabilitation program run by Mr Devin's dealership and advocated by Tiffany Stevens. Miss Stevens' teen shelter building project was destroyed by a suspicious fire last night. Neither Mr Devin's family nor Miss

Stevens were available for comment today, but we have been informed that Mr Devin is co-operating with police in their enquiry. More on that story later … Now to a —'

TJ turned off the television and tossed the remote onto the coffee table. What had Scott seen in that list that had made the shutters slam shut? Her heart could not … would not … accept that he had somehow been involved in Tiny's death and the subsequent fire. What possible motive could he have? He'd embraced the program, involved himself in the building project and mentored both boys without a hint of adversity.

Cold crept up her spine as the puzzle pieces started to fall into place to form a picture she wished she couldn't see. Scott's buying a struggling business on the opposite side of the country with a direct link to drug rehabilitation. The controversy over Serena Snow and her case against him for harassment. Had that court case been a smoke screen?

Serena showing up in town with an obvious connection to Gino Bennetti, who himself had questionable ties to the underground. Was Scott a pawn in the game or a player?

Sarge grumbled as he stood to stretch and shake the sleep from his body. He sat and stared at her a moment with his sad brown eyes before sitting down and placing his large head on her lap. TJ rubbed his ears.

'Looks like it's only you and me now, buddy.'

Sarge answered with a yawn and wandered over to the French doors leading to the veranda. TJ stood and stretched her aching muscles before opening the door to let him out for a run.

'Don't wander too far away from the house, Sarge.'

After the events of last night, she was reluctant to have to go searching for him if he decided to take off. Her once safe haven now felt empty, dark and threatening. Maybe it was time to give up. Maybe she had to accept that she couldn't make a difference.

No. That would be admitting defeat. TJ Stevens was no quitter. She would have to find another way. For Tiny, Marty, Luke and Connor, and all the others to come.

She sighed as her mobile phone vibrated on the coffee table. The screen flashed brightly in the dim light of the room. Picking it up she scanned the screen. Rose.

'Hi Rose,' she said.

'Hello love.' Rose's voice was thick with tears. 'How are you holding up?'

'A little numb.'

'Yes, I understand. You don't believe all this nonsense do you?'

'I don't know what to believe right now.'

'We've been told to stay indoors, otherwise we'd come over. Are you okay alone over there?'

'I'll be fine, Rose. I have Sarge.' She heaved a sigh of relief as the big dog wandered back in through the open door. TJ walked back over to close and lock it. For the first time in the history of Rowley's Gumnut Cottage, she drew the curtains on the twinkling lights of the hills.

'He didn't do it, TJ.'

'My heart knows that, but my head is telling me different.'

'Then follow your heart. I'm sure the police will have answers soon. Mark Johnson is a good detective. He'll find the truth.'

'Yes.' She hoped with all her heart he would.

Chapter Eighteen

onday morning came around too soon for TJ. What would she find down the hill at the dealership this morning? With Scott in custody, what would happen to the business? She opened the door of the shed, thankful that it had survived the fire with only a few black scars where the flames had licked at the foundations. If she'd lost Bruce too, she would have lost everything. But there stood the shiny FJ Holden ute, unscathed. A sign of hope amongst the ruins of her dreams.

The cloud of despair that had settled around her shoulders lifted a little as she opened the door.

'Come on, Sarge, in you get.' There was no harm in taking him along with her today. At least he wouldn't be home alone. Her mobile rang in the pocket of her jeans.

She fished it out to look at the screen. Private number. Frowning, she answered it. 'Hello?'

'The fire was only the beginning. Rebuild and you're next.' The sexless, tinny voice echoed from the speaker into the misty morning air.

Anger warred with fear as TJ tensed at the threat. Anger won. 'Fuck you, you witless bastard. You want me? Come and get me. I'll be waiting.' She hung up and tossed the phone onto the seat.

Bile rose in her throat, but she forced it back down. Stupid. How could she be so stupid? Sometimes her mouth engaged before her brain. She'd given an arsonist and possible murderer an open invitation.

Sliding onto the driver's seat, she secured the dog's harness and connected it to the seatbelt. 'That was a bloody silly thing to do, wasn't it, Sarge?'

She started the engine, shifted into drive and carefully manoeuvred the car out of the shed. Her hands shook a little as she stopped to put it in neutral and got out to close the shed door.

Back in the car, she negotiated the blackened driveway onto the Brookton Highway before picking up the discarded phone and dialling Mark Johnson's number.

'Detective Mark Johnson.' The deep, serious tone in his voice was oddly reassuring.

'Mark, it's TJ.'

'I know. You're in my phone under *Trouble*. I hope you're on hands-free. I can hear traffic.'

She smiled. 'I have my hands a little full right now.'

'No kidding. What's up?'

'I received a phone call this morning. Apparently the caller wants me dead too.'

'What did he say?'

'That I'm next if I rebuild. It sounded like the voice was disguised, like a recording or something.'

His voice turned to stone. 'Where are you now?'

'On my way to work.'

'I'll see you there. We're on our way there to check up on a few leads.'

'What will happen to the business?'

'Business as usual until we find anything that confirms Scott's involvement. If that happens, everything will be seized by the courts and all his assets frozen.'

'And we'll all be out of a job.'

'Pretty much. I'll get to the bottom of it.'

'I know you will.' She flicked her indicator on to turn right onto Albany Highway. 'Do you really believe he's involved?'

Mark's pause weighed heavily in the cab of the ute. 'You know I can't say.'

'I know. It was unfair of me to ask.'

'The notebook and the list are proving useful evidence. Tiny was a clever boy.'

'Yes, he was. Pity he wasn't clever enough to stay away from it all together.'

'Kids do silly things.'

'Silly things get them killed.' She backed off the accelerator as a teenage driver with probationary plates displayed in his back window sped past to cut back into the lane in front of her. 'Case in point. Bloody P-platers!'

Mark chuckled. 'Try to stay out of trouble until you get here. I'll be waiting.'

She hung up as she indicated her turn into the dealership parking lot. Bruce slid home neatly into a vacant bay, and she turned off the engine. Sarge hung his head out the open window and barked loudly as TJ unclipped his harness from the seatbelt. She ruffled his neck.

'It's okay, big fella. You can stand down.'

He whined and nudged her arm as if to hurry her along. Her hand paused on the door handle as she saw Scott standing at the window of his office. With a sigh, she opened the door and got out, followed closely by Sarge's bulk. She hooked a finger on the loop of his harness to stop him taking off and scaring the customers.

Marty was the first to spot her from the workshop and he jogged over.

'Hey,' he said by way of greeting, his fist held out for a knuckle bump.

'Hey.' TJ met his knuckle bump with her own. 'I guess you heard about the fire?'

'Yeah. Shit luck.' He fished 20c out of his pocket and dropped it in her outstretched hand. 'What's gonna happen now?'

'I don't know.' The hopelessness of the reply echoed in the parking lot. 'I guess we'll decide once we have the report from the fire.'

'Sucks.'

'Yes it does. How are you doing?'

'Yeah, I'm good. Just pissed about this whole thing.'

'Are you staying out of trouble?'

Yep. I'm done with that shit now. I promised Mum.'

'That's great, Marty. Are you staying on at home?'

'Yeah. Mum said I could move back in. But I have to stay clean.'

'And you will.' TJ punched his arm.

He surprised her by hugging her tightly. 'Thanks TJ. I would never have gotten this far without you … and Mr D.' He let her go and stepped back. 'Why are the cops here?'

'Long story. I'll tell you and the others what's going on when I have more facts. Right now, all we have is clues.'

'Okay. Tony's got things under control. Detective Johnson said to tell you to come to Mr D's office when you're ready.'

'Thanks, mate. Can you take Sarge out back and give him some water?'

'Sure thing.' He took the leash from TJ and hooked it into the clip of the harness. 'Come, Sarge.'

With only the slightest hesitation, Sarge trotted after Marty as TJ made her way inside. She waved to the workshop boys through the observation window. They stood lined up at the clock machine waiting to start the day. In the reception area, the service advisors attended the customers, whose curious glances kept swinging to the police cars parked in the lot. They would have seen the news, heard the rumours. Things wouldn't remain a secret for much longer. It would become the talk down at the local pub over a few beers, the gossip in the queue at the post office, the whispers on the bus into the city.

'It's okay. It's business as usual, Mrs Thomas. The police are here to do a routine investigation.' TJ reassured one of their regulars who wondered out loud whether she should leave her car here after all.

Would things ever be okay again? Scott's door loomed in the gloomy corridor. The office staff would be arriving soon, and the administration department on her left would become a hive of activity ... and gossip. Squaring her shoulders, she pushed open the door to Scott's office.

Mark looked up from the computer screen he studied, pen in hand poised above his notebook.

'Morning, TJ. Take a seat.'

'Hi, Mark. Scott.'

Her gaze settled on his back, stiff and straight, his shoulders squarely set, ready to take the load. He didn't turn around, but he wasn't cuffed either. He acknowledged her greeting with a silent nod.

'So, tell me about the phone call.' Mark drew her attention away as rejection squeezed painfully at her heart.

'Not much to tell really. He said that if I rebuild, I'll be next.'

'What makes you think the voice was male?'

'I don't. It could be male or female, but it was tinny. Like a recording through a synthesiser or one of those kid's masks that make you sound like Darth Vader.'

'What did you say?'

TJ shrugged. 'I told him to come and get me. Then I hung up.' She sensed rather than saw Scott turn from the window, felt his gaze burn on her face. Good, he was angry. She preferred anger. It was better than the cold wall he'd put up.

Mark pinched the bridge of his nose and squeezed his eyes shut. 'Jesus, TJ. Why do you have to be such a little scrapper? Couldn't you just put the phone down like a normal person?'

'No. Where would the fun be in that?'

'Fun? You think this is a joke?' Scott stalked over to where she sat and hauled her up out of the chair. His fingers bit into her upper arms as his eyes burned on hers.

TJ met his glare with equal fire. 'I've just lost everything I've worked so damn hard for. If whoever did this wants to come after me, I say let them come. I won't go down without a fight!'

'You won't be alive to fight!'

'Is that a threat?'

Mark cleared his throat. 'Put her down, Scott.' He leaned back in the chair and looked at them thoughtfully. 'I might leave you two alone for a moment. Try not to shed too much blood. One murder investigation is about as much as I can handle right now.'

With his gaze anchoring hers, Scott set TJ on her feet and loosened his grip on her arms. 'Thanks, Mark.'

'Yeah, thanks Mark …' Sarcasm dripped from her tone.

As the door closed behind the detective, Scott rubbed her upper arms where his fingers had left red imprints. 'Sorry, I didn't mean to hurt you. This isn't a game, TJ.'

'I'm aware of that.'

'Give it up, please. Even if only until this case is settled.'

'I can't. What happens to the likes of Marty, Luke and Connor while I sit back and let some greedy drug lords take everything away from us? What will it take to end this? Nothing because it will *never* end, Scott. If they catch whoever did this, there'll be someone else to take their place. It's a fight I'll keep on fighting, no matter how hopeless it seems at times.'

'Until what? Until they kill you too? Until they take everything you have left?'

'If that's what it takes. So, tell your little girlfriend and her cronies to come and get me. I'm waiting.' She punctuated the last word with a stab of her forefinger on his chest.

He stilled her attack on his chest. 'Do you believe I had something to do with it?'

For a moment, TJ stared into his eyes, searching for honesty, integrity, and all the good things she'd learned about the man who'd shared her bed. If she'd been *that* wrong about him, her dick radar needed serious calibration.

'No.'

'That's all I need to know.' He lifted his hand to trace her face. 'I need you to trust me, TJ. Now more than ever.'

Her hands crept up his chest, touched the cords of his neck and the stubble on his jaw. He was tired. Judging from the bloodshot eyes, he'd had even less sleep than she'd had. For a moment she held his gaze and read what was clear in their depth. 'I have no choice, Scott. You made me fall in love with you.'

His kiss was soft and gentle, little more than a

fleeting touch that broke her heart with each sweep of his lips.

'Okay, kids. Break it up …' Mark's voice interrupted as they slowly stepped apart. 'It's time to go, Scott.'

Scott set her away from him with a sigh. 'It will be okay.'

She wanted to believe him with every inch of her soul. 'I've got to get back to work now. I have a shop to run.' Her hands slid from his chest as she pushed away and walked to the door.

'And TJ?' Mark's voice stopped her. 'Stay out of trouble. At least until we can solve this case.'

TJ smiled. 'I'll try, but I can't make any promises.'

Chapter Nineteen

Three weeks later, TJ sat on her veranda, beer in hand as she watched the contractor and his mini excavator scrape up the rubble from the fire and dump it in the back of a trailer.

A completely new beginning. All that remained of the old cabins now was what she'd come to think of as Tiny's Chimney. The new brick walls they'd built had been unstable from the heat of the fire and had to be pulled down. She'd decided to make a completely new start.

The site would become a garden, a meeting place she'd open to teens. Tiny's chimney would house an inbuilt gas barbeque. He'd like that. Picnic tables and benches, a site to pitch tents and camp out. The council had agreed to sponsor activities in a partnership with the Police Citizens and Youth Club.

Another sponsor had promised them a graffiti wall where teens could express their emotions in paint — no spray cans — only brushes. And when the wall was full, their anger and frustration forgotten, they could whitewash it and start again. Layer after layer of paint and emotion … a cleansing ritual.

Sheila was home in the shed next to Bruce, her engine on a pallet next to her. With her engine and transmission removed to make her lighter, they'd found a towing contractor with a racing car trailer that could make the steep climb up the hill that a flatbed truck couldn't.

Every weekend, Marty, Connor and Luke came up, pitched their tent under the gum tree by the creek and spent their days overhauling the engine or stripping out her interior in preparation for restoration. A few of Tiny's possessions had place of honour on a shelf in the shed — his coffee cup, a handful of tools. The boys were constructing a box frame to display them in. When it was finished, it would go up on the wall at the back of the shed. All they were waiting for was Tiny's notebook to come home. That would be the centrepiece of their tribute.

TJ thought of the band equipment donated by the local second-hand shop and the area at the back of the shed that was set to become a recording studio. The plans lay on the table in front of her. A little sound deadener on the walls to protect the neighbours and a set of earplugs for her and Sarge and they'd be right. All that was missing was Scott.

Scott. The investigation had gone into lockdown with a total press ban. Since it was business as usual down at the dealership, she assumed they'd found nothing there to link Scott to the murder or the fire. Why then was he still in police custody?

There'd been no more threatening phone calls and no more incidents at the property. She wondered if that was due to the strong police presence, the off-duty cops who came up to mentor the boys. Or perhaps it was that word had got around that she had no plans to rebuild the shelter. Maybe they didn't see a garden as a big threat to their trade.

Wheels scrunched and an engine heaved as a car made its way up her freshly compacted gravel drive. Sarge sat to attention with a single bark. TJ rubbed his neck and placed her bottle on the table next to her chair. She stood and stretched.

The house was so quiet she couldn't sleep at night. How things had changed. A soft smile caressed her lips as the music from the shed pumped up a bit and the boys belted out an AC/DC favourite. The amplifier squealed in protest. TJ saw Mark wince as he stepped out of his unmarked car.

'I'm surprised the local police station hasn't been inundated with noise pollution complaints,' he commented half-jokingly as he made his way up the stairs.

'It's Saturday, they're not open. The neighbours have agreed to two hours practice per day during daylight hours until the sound proofing goes in. The vote's still out as to what happens after that.'

'Hopefully by that time they'll have learnt how to adjust the amp.'

She laughed. 'What brings you up here?'

'Good news and bad news.'

'I can handle the good news but the bad news? I'm not so sure. Can I get you a drink?'

'No, I have to get back into town. I have a desk piled high with paperwork and a case that has more red herrings than answers.'

'No worries. So, give me the bad news first.'

He ran a hand through his short, blond hair and removed his sunglasses to perch them on top of his head in the newly created spikes. What a shame he wasn't her kind of guy, she thought. He was damn good looking. One day he'd make some girl very lucky. Just not this girl. Sky blue eyes met hers with a serious look.

'We're no closer to finding who is responsible for Tiny's death. I can tell you that the fire was no accident. My guess is you knew that already. The notebook and the list you found have been valuable clues, but not enough to point the finger squarely at anyone.'

'Where does that leave Scott?'

'That's the good news.' He turned toward the car as the passenger door opened. 'He's free to go.'

TJ's heart flip-flopped as Scott got out and walked slowly toward them. He looked tired, worn out. The stubble was gone, his clothes were fresh, and his dark hair glistened in the sunlight. The Scott who loped toward her now was a shadow of the one who'd left. Gone was the cockiness, the self-assuredness in his step. Instead, fingers hooked into the top of the front pockets of his jeans, he seemed unsure of his welcome.

For a moment he hesitated, his attention turned to where the excavator dropped a load into the trailer with a *thunk*. Brick against metal, a resounding reminder of what had taken place weeks before. He didn't look as if he needed or wanted reminding.

What if this was the end? What if he didn't want to be here anymore? Would he head back to the east coast to start over again? A pang of regret gripped her heart. Was it over before it began? Her heart fluttered back to life as he focused his gaze on her, held her eyes with his until he reached the steps. She stood poised on the last step, her knuckles white as she twisted her hands together.

'TJ.'

'Scott.' The ache in her heart spread to her throat and made her eyes sting with tears.

'Well, I'll leave you two alone then. Scott will fill you in, TJ.'

'Sure, Mark. Thanks.' She dragged her gaze from Scott's and leaned forward to kiss Mark's cheek.

With a pat on the back for Scott and a wave to both, Mark got in his car and drove away. For a long moment, TJ stared at Scott, taking in the tight lines around his mouth, the tired wariness in his eyes.

'Would you like a beer?'

'Cheers.'

'Come on up and take a seat. I'll be out with one in a minute. Sarge, look who's home.' She turned and headed up the stairs as Sarge came bounding around the corner. At the top of the stairs, she paused to watch Scott go down on his haunches to give his dog a belly rub. No doubting he'd missed his dog. But what about her and Marty?

When she came out a few minutes later with a cold beer in her hands, Scott was at the veranda railing looking out across the valley. He turned at the sound of her footsteps and accepted the bottle she held out to him. Eyes on hers, he drank deeply.

'God, that tastes good.'

TJ levered herself up on the railing and swung her legs over the other side to face the same view he'd been admiring.

'So, you're off the hook?' She kept her face turned to the valley.

A sigh and shuffle before the glass bottle clinked down on the rail, which moved beneath her as he hoisted himself up and swung his legs over too. His warm thigh pressed against hers. She'd missed those subtle touches that sent the blood pulsing through her.

'Yes. They found nothing to tie me to any of it. The tipoff they received was that my businesses were being used to launder drug money. Since the addresses of two of those dealerships were on Tiny's list, it looked a little suspicious.'

He offered her the beer. She looked at the bottle and took it from him. Their fingers brushed and she raised her eyes to his face. Dark eyes stared back at her, searching. For what?

'Do they know where the tip off came from?'

'No, but they have their suspicions.'

'Why were the addresses of your dealerships on Tiny's list?'

He took a while to answer.

'Because they were being used. I've handed all the evidence I have over to them.'

'So how come you're in the clear?'

'Because my signature isn't on any of the deals. The money was being laundered through used car sales. The customers would come in and pay cash for older models. The investigation turned up that those cars were then traded or sold on a few months later.'

'Whose signature was on those deals?' Even as she

asked the question, TJ had a sinking feeling she already knew the answer.

'Serena's.'

She watched his throat work as he swallowed a mouthful of beer.

'She set you up? The bitch.'

A hint of a smile turned up the corners of his mouth. 'Aah, I've missed you, Tiger.' He bumped her shoulder with his. 'Yes, she set me up. A continuation of her vendetta.'

'What happens now?'

'The focus of the investigation is now on the link between Serena and Gino Bennetti. As it turns out, Serena is Paul Price's niece. His nightclub was used as the headquarters. Apparently Mark has video evidence and a set of dodgy books from Price's arrest that ties in with some of the clues in Tiny's notebook. The problem is that the chief suspect happens to be a lawyer.'

'Bennetti?' She shivered. 'His son, Luke, is up in the shed with the boys now. Poor kid. The man's a pig.'

'A pig we hope will soon be off the streets. If they can make their case stick.' He swung his legs back over the railing and dropped onto the veranda deck. With a flick of his wrist, he tossed the empty bottle into the recycle bin in the corner.

TJ turned to face him but stayed on the railing, her hands gripping the edge. 'So, where've you been for three weeks?'

'Helping them with their investigation. I've spent three weeks sleeping on an uncomfortable couch in Harold Jones's apartment. That man snores like a goddam freight train!'

'Why didn't you call?'

'I couldn't. Not until we'd figured out who set me up. This goes a whole lot deeper than Serena's vendetta against me. They thought it might be safer if I didn't come home.'

Home. 'Is this home for you now? Or will you be moving on to another challenge?'

He moved to stand in front of her and reached out a hand to cup her cheek. 'I think I've found a challenge right here that will keep me busy for a very long time.'

Her heart skipped a beat as he whispered the words against her lips and his hand skimmed up her neck and into her hair.

TJ closed her eyes and revelled in the sensations his fingers created as they massaged her scalp, applying pressure to inch her forward. She sank into his kiss, her arms wrapped around his neck as she wriggled closer, desperate for contact. Still not close enough, she wrapped her legs around his hips and stretched her torso against him like a satisfied cat.

Scott's hand slipped from behind her head to trail down her back and pressed her closer still. Muscular rigidity met soft buttery curves, as he lifted her off the railing. Her legs tightened around him, the thin cotton of her track pants no barrier against his need. She rubbed against him, satisfied with the low growl from his throat.

The hand on her back moved to hoist her up away from temptation and caressed her bottom. 'Easy, Tiger,' he said breaking the kiss. 'How long will the boys be kept amused by that racket?' He tilted his head toward the shed where the boys were torturing yet another rock song.

'Until their curfew ends in about an hour.'

'And the guy on the mini excavator?'

'He'll leave when he's done.'

'So, have you got anything planned for the next hour or so?'

TJ smiled, loosened her legs and slid down his body. 'Oh, I think I can find something to keep me amused.' Her finger trailed down the line of buttons on his shirt and she pressed a kiss at the V of the opening. 'Do you think we've done enough to keep the boys out of trouble?'

'It's a war that will never end. All we can do is fight it, one battle at a time.' His lips brushed her head. 'Together. Mark is doing everything he can to get to the bottom of this and crack the drug ring. We'll keep doing our bit. Later, you and the boys can give me an update on what you've got planned. But right now?' Strong fingers feathered up her spine and lightly brushed against her breast. 'Right now, I've got another tiger to tame.'

TJ offered no resistance as he swept her up and over his shoulder in a fireman's lift. The view wasn't bad from there, she thought. His jeans moulded him perfectly, the muscles clenching and loosening with each stride into the house and up toward the bedroom. One arm braced against his warm back, she allowed the other to slip under the waistband to caress the firm skin underneath.

He patted her bottom as he manoeuvred through the door and kicked it closed behind them. Gently he lowered her onto the bed and knelt over her. Her hands crept up to loosen the buttons on his shirt. He shrugged it off, dipping his head to kiss her nose, her eyes and finally, her lips.

'I love you, Tiffany-Jane.'

'And I love you … but you're still a pompous arse.'

He smiled at the reminder of the first time they met and spent the next hour proving her wrong.

Mark Johnson sat at his desk with the evidence that had begun to mount, along with a string of suspects. Insufficient evidence for a conviction, but enough to build a case and point the finger squarely in the direction of Gino Bennetti being involved. All he needed was a crackdown to catch him red-handed with his hand in the pie. Unfortunately, the lawyer was clever enough to remain on the right side of the very thin line of his association with the underworld of drugs and criminal activities. But even lawyers made mistakes eventually and, when Gino Bennetti made his, Mark would be waiting.

Silenced (Unfinished Business Book 3)

Want to know what happens next? Join DSS Mark Johnson and his partner, Harold, as they continue their investigation.

Silenced (Unfinished Business Book 3)
   by Juanita Kees

Overwhelmed in the aftermath of her husband's death, Lily Bennetti navigates protecting her teenage son from his father's criminal legacy and the dangers that continue to stalk them. The secrets she keeps come at a high cost. If the detective on the case figures out the truth about her connection to a cold case murder, she stands to lose everything she has left.

When Mark Johnson delves deeper into his ongoing investigation of the murder of Tiny Watts, the last person he expects to be interviewing for it is a crime boss' widow. His gut tells him she knows more than she's letting on. Her bruises tell a different story. The way she defends her son suggests that the threat runs even deeper than her scars. He's determined to bring the notorious crime gang ruling the streets to justice, but at what cost?

Chapter 1

Lily Bennetti's head swam. Red spots danced in her vision and an agonising throb beat at the top of her skull. She lifted a hand to touch the tender spot. Her fingers came away sticky with blood. Slowly, painfully, she lowered her hand to the cream, plush pile carpet. Her palm brushed across broken glass. The coffee table — she'd fallen when Gino had pushed her away, hit her head on it.

'You dumb arse piece of *shit*!' Gino's voice pierced her thoughts, dark and threatening, somehow scarier than the yelling she vaguely remembered from earlier. Luke's response was muffled. Through the haze of pain, she focused on the figures standing in front of her — one big and bulky, the other a mere featherweight.

Gino stood, feet apart and menacing as he anchored

Luke up against the far wall, his stance way meaner than the words he hissed through his teeth.

Luke gripped Gino's wrists in an effort to force his meaty hands from his neck. The terror in her son's body language sent fear barrelling through her. Bile rose in her throat. *Dear God.* Gino was going to kill Luke.

No. Lily stumbled to her feet. Blood rushed to her head, dizziness had her crashing to her knees. Desperation chased away the fear. She had to get to Luke. Her jaw ached where Gino had smacked her. She tasted the coppery tang of blood on her tongue where her teeth had sunk into the soft flesh of her lip. *No more.* She dragged her aching body up, using the sofa for support. As the little colour left in Luke's face drained away, Lily drew on all the strength she had left. Saving her son was all that mattered.

'*Stop*, Gino.' Desperation rang in her voice as she raised it over her husband's. Silence fell heavily on the lounge room. She staggered protectively toward Luke. Gino dropped his hands to his sides, fists clenched.

Lily gripped the torn sleeve of her son's shirt. Angry red welts criss-crossed the pale teenage flesh underneath. Then she saw it. The gun in Luke's hand pointed at his father's heart. 'Jesus, Luke. Don't do it. It's not worth it.'

'No, Mum. I'm done. Done taking his crap.' His voice was gritty. The purple marks at his throat evidence of the pressure his father had placed on his windpipe.

Lily placed a shaking hand over Luke's equally unsteady one. 'This isn't the way.'

Gino snorted. 'He doesn't have the guts for it, Liliana. He's weak. Takes after his mother. A no good, lazy sonofabitch. He doesn't have the spine to pull the trigger.'

Gino lunged forward to grip his son's wrist. It happened in slow motion, the way she'd seen it in movies. A shot rang out and surprise registered on Gino's face before his body crumpled to the floor with a bullet in his chest. Dark red blood seeped into the cream carpet as his life drained away. Silence stretched as Lily and Luke stood, the sound of the shot reverberating in their ears. The gun slipped from Luke's nerveless hands.

Detective Mark Johnson closed the notebook and turned it over in his hands, the words still clouding his mind.

GB came to work today, cornered me in the parking lot. I'm pissed off. I thought they'd leave me alone after the last bust. Someone's going to get hurt. I think it could be me. How did I get into this? I want out but I know they won't let me. I'm not scared to die. It's the other boys in the gang I'm worried about. Luke, Marty and Connor. Luke is too close. He and his mum are sporting shiners again. GB is getting crazier. I hate that he takes it out on his own family.

Cleverly concealed in the graffitied cover were clues that teenage gang leader, Tiny Watts, was murdered. All they had to do was prove it and find his killer. It should have been an open and shut case; a gang of troubled kids, a drug deal gone wrong. Instead, the more dirt he uncovered, the deeper the roots went.

Tiny had left a notebook of clues with keywords hidden in the bricks he'd drawn on the cover. Matching people to initials had created a jigsaw puzzle with too many missing pieces. At the same time, it connected the dots between three key players consistently. The initials SS, GB and NA appeared in almost every sketch, disguised by graffiti or imbedded in objects.

Having read a chunk of the notebook Tiny had left in his room at the shelter, Mark was convinced that GB was Gino Bennetti. The prominent gangland lawyer certainly didn't have a squeaky-clean record. But how was he involved? Who was he protecting? The video evidence they'd gathered from the convention centre parking garage proved his car was there at the time Tiny disappeared. But there was no proof he'd snatched the boy.

'Hey, Buddy, put your toys away.' Mark's partner, Harold Jones, stuck his head around the door. 'We've got ourselves a murder in interview room one.'

Mark shoved the notebook into the evidence bag. 'They're bloody dropping like flies.' Tired, he lowered his feet off the desk and straightened. The last few months had exhausted him. Trouble had struck way too close to home for his liking. His sister's daughter was kidnapped and held for ransom by her stepfather, Paul Price. Paul had owed money to Gino Bennetti. The link between her kidnapping and Tiny's gang had grown stronger with each piece of new evidence that came to light and he didn't like the path it was taking.

'Boy aged seventeen. Neighbours heard shouting, like a fight. Loads of thumping. They heard the woman crying, shouting at them to stop. A shot, a scream and… nothing. Neighbour called it in. She was too scared to go over there.' Harold dropped the manila file on his desk. 'It looks like the boy killed his father.'

Mark flicked through the scribbled case notes, his eyes coming to rest on the victim's name. 'Fuck!'

'That's what I thought you'd say.'

'I guess that takes Gino Bennetti off our list of suspects to interview in the Watts murder. Tell me more.'

Harold shrugged. 'The boy's not talking. They're both pretty messed up.'

'They?' Mark frowned at Harold as he closed the file and stood.

'His mum's in there with him. Boy's name is Luke. He's one of the Tag Raiders.'

Tiredness fled and Mark's back stiffened. 'The boy named Luke — the boy Tiny mentioned in his notes — is Gino Bennetti's *son*?'

'They don't call you fuckin' super sleuth for nothin', do they?' Harold mocked.

'The lines are becoming very blurred, Harold.' Mark waved the file at the door. 'Let's go talk to the kid.'

As he walked through the door of interview room one, his gaze fell on Gino Bennetti's widow. Lily Bennetti looked like a bedraggled angel who'd been to Hell and back on a bumpy ride. Long, honey-blonde hair lay tangled around her shoulders. Even streaked with blood from the cut on her left cheek, it shone like a halo under the hot, industrial lighting. She turned to face him, and his breath hitched in his throat. Watery blue eyes blazed red from under swollen lids, a dark bruise bloomed on her right cheek and her top lip swelled around a split in the middle.

Anger churned in his gut. If the man wasn't already dead, he'd fucking kill him himself. No one deserved to take a beating like this. He turned his gaze to the boy, watched him flinch as he pulled out a chair and it scraped against the concrete floor. Mark noticed the scars on his arms first, exposed by the ripped sleeves of his shirt, and made a mental note. Drugs, self-harm or abuse? Luke's hands trembled on the table, bloodied and bruised, knuckles swollen and split. He'd given Gino a good bashing, but by the look of his left cheek and eye, he'd been dealt a few nasty blows too.

Mark sat in the chair and faced them. Lily Bennetti looked nothing at all like the photos he'd seen in Gino

Bennetti's file. Gone was the confident, smiling young woman on the arm of her good-looking Italian husband. In her place was a broken doll, her silky pale skin a patchwork of angry welts and bruises, her shoulders hunched as she hugged her arms tightly against her stomach. He ignored the tug at his heart, the urge to comfort her, to tell her it would be alright.

'Mrs Bennetti, I'm Detective Mark Johnson,' he began. 'Do you have any objection to me asking your son a few questions?' Lily shook her head but didn't look up, so he tried again. 'I'm sorry, but you have to answer the question for the record.' He tried to keep his voice neutral, but gentleness crept in as her eyelids flickered.

The pain it caused her to speak was obvious. This time she raised her eyes to his. 'No.' She winced as she touched her lip below the split.

'Thank you.' He wanted to reach out to touch her hand reassuringly, but she'd clenched them tightly in her lap. He turned to the boy. 'Luke, would you like to tell me what happened?'

Silence met his question and the boy continued to stare at his hands. Mark sighed. It was going to be like pulling teeth. Lily unclenched her hands and laid one over Luke's with a squeeze. He pulled away with a jerk and sunk deeper into his seat.

'It's okay, tell him.' She withdrew her hands and clenched them in her lap.

Luke's jaw flexed as he fought his inner battle. Mark watched. Body language was a dead giveaway. What this boy would say came from deep beyond the physical injuries.

With a sigh, Luke sat up in his chair. He kept his eyes on the table, but he unclenched his hands as he began to speak. 'Dad and I got into a fight. He called me a dumb arse piece of shit.'

'Why were you arguing?'

'I told him I was done. I didn't want to work for him anymore. He got mad.'

'Done with what?'

'Running his deliveries.'

Mark made a note. Gino Bennetti was a criminal lawyer. What deliveries could his son possibly do for him? A question for later, he thought as it raised a red flag in his gut. 'What happened then?'

'He grabbed me by the throat and pushed me up against the wall. Mum tried to stop him.'

Mark's gaze flicked to Lily's hands as she twisted them nervously. His eyes on her face, he asked Luke, 'What did your dad do then?'

Luke looked at his mother for a long moment, his eyes glittering with tears he struggled to hold back. 'He punched her in the face, and she fell backwards onto the coffee table. He knocked her unconscious! He could have killed her. I'm not sorry the bastard's dead.'

'*Luke.*' Lily's voice broke over his name.

'It's true, Mum!' He raised his voice and his mother flinched. 'He treated us like shit! Made us do stuff that —'

'What did he make you do?' Mark encouraged when Luke's words ended abruptly. If the boy clammed up now, it could be a while before they drew the truth out of him. Experience had taught him to strike while the adrenalin was high. 'Luke, we're here to help you. What work did you do for him?'

Luke paused and looked at his mother for a long moment. Silence spread in the interview room like a dark and gloomy cloud. At Lily's nod, he continued, 'I delivered parcels for him. I didn't want to do it anymore, not after Tiny Watts…died.'

Mark straightened in his seat and narrowed his eyes at the hesitation in the boy's voice. 'So, you and Tiny Watts were friends?'

'We were in the same gang. The Tag Raiders.'

'What was in the parcels you delivered for your father?'

As Luke took a breath to continue, the door to the interview room flew open and banged against the wall. 'Shut up, you idiot. Detective Johnson, my client will not be answering any further questions.'

Mark was on his feet immediately. The man reeked of slimy, no-good lawyering. His expensive suit and shoes, gold watch, dark looks and meaty fists screamed *underworld* as he thumped his Armani briefcase on the table next to Luke. Luke and Lily stood and backed away. Fear flashed across their faces. Lily gripped Luke's upper arm, her knuckles white.

'No!' She squared her shoulders, her spine ramrod straight, fear in her eyes, determination in her voice. 'No.'

'Yes!' He turned to Mark. 'I'm Gino's business partner from Albero and Bennetti lawyers. Nic Albero. I'd say it was a pleasure, but I'd be lying. Is my client under arrest?'

'He's not your client.' Lily's quiet voice shook.

'Don't be a fool, Liliana!' The big man took a step toward them. 'The boy is *not* in a position to argue. Neither are you.' He flashed them a warning look that fell just short of mean.

Harold stepped forward from where he'd stood, quietly observing the interruption. 'Since there would appear to be a conflict of interest here, the court will assign a lawyer for Luke if you prefer, Mrs Bennetti.'

'Conflict of interest?' Albero's outrage echoed off the concrete walls. He moved surprisingly fast for such a bulky man as he spun toward Mark and Harold.

Harold stepped between Albero and Lily, pushing him away a couple of steps. 'As the victim's business partner, I doubt the boy would get a fair defence. This is a murder case, Mr Albero, and you have too much to gain if the boy is found guilty.'

'That's bullshit and you know it,' Albero sneered.

'Come to think of it, how did you know we had him in custody?' Mark asked.

Albero hesitated, his eyes shifting to the wall. 'It's on the news.'

Mark stepped forward, arms across the expanse of his chest. 'There's an embargo on the press releasing any details on the shooting because the suspect is under age. Try again.'

He'd spent enough years on the force to recognise Albero's type, even if the lawyer's reputation didn't speak for itself. Bugging phones, tracing calls and intercepting police data were all part and parcel of his defence tactics.

'*I'm* his lawyer!' Albero ignored the underlying accusation.

'No!' said Lily. This time her voice was strong and confident. 'Luke will have a court lawyer.' She pushed Luke behind her and stepped around Harold. 'We don't need your…services, Nic.'

'You're making a *big* mistake.'

'Get out.' Her shaking hands belied the deadly calm of her voice.

Albero's eyes narrowed on hers. 'You'll regret this, Liliana.' He turned and walked away. The door slammed behind his departing bulk with the force of a gunshot and Lily Bennetti, tired, battered and broken, crumpled to the concrete floor.

Chapter 1

Lily awoke to the clinical white walls of the hospital emergency department, the beep of equipment and the echo of footsteps in a corridor. Confused, she lay a moment trying to get her bearings. Her heart pounded to life as she remembered — Nic Albero.

'Luke!' she cried and struggled to sit up. God, her ribs ached, and her head pounded in rhythm with her heart. The needle in her hand twisted painfully and she looked around to see it attached to a drip.

A gentle hand touched her arm and she jerked away. Wincing, she turned her head to see Detective Mark Johnson straddling a chair next to her. Arms folded along the backrest, chin resting on muscular forearms, his short, dark blond hair was messy, and he looked… tired. Deep grey eyes studied her from under brows a shade darker than his hair, his gaze intense. Lily felt she should be intimidated by it, yet somehow it was reassuring, comforting.

'You and Luke are in hospital. When you fainted, Luke got a little upset. The doctor says you might have concussion.'

'Where's Luke?' she asked, her voice fringed with panic.

Big, tanned arms unfolded, and he waved a long-fingered hand at the curtains around the next cubicle.

'He's on the other side of those. They've got him under sedation. It's okay, Mrs Bennetti, you're both safe.'

She fell back against the pillows and closed her eyes. 'Safe? I don't think you understand, Detective.'

'Help me understand. Why are you so terrified of Nic Albero?'

'Nic isn't one to take no for an answer.'

'He threatened you.'

'Yes.' Her fingers tightened on the bed sheets. 'I defied him. Broke the family code. Nic is...was... Gino's cousin.'

Now he'd be out for blood. They were as good as dead. They knew too much and with Gino gone and no one to keep them in check, Nic knew they were an even bigger risk to his operation. She turned to look at the man sitting in the chair. It would be so good to share her burden with someone she could trust. For a long time, she'd suspected her husband was involved in the underworld of drug trafficking and crime. What she hadn't expected was that he'd drag their son there with him.

'Why don't you want him to defend your son?'

'Because I don't trust him.'

If Luke went to prison for murder — even detention in juvie while he waited for his case to be heard — Albero's thugs would get to him, and he'd be dead in weeks. They were sitting ducks. There was nowhere to run. She closed her eyes as tears squeezed from beneath her lids and ran down her cheeks.

'Mrs Bennetti…Lily…if there's something you know about Nic Albero, you need to tell me. If you want a fair trial for your son, you can't keep information to yourself.'

'I can't…' Luke wouldn't get a fair trial at all if the police found out he was in the car when Tiny was murdered. He was a witness, an accessory. The evidence would send him to prison for good. 'I can't.'

'You have my word. We will make sure you and your son are safe during this investigation.' The deep, soothing voice did nothing to calm her nerves.

'What use is your word, Detective? It's no protection against a car bomb, or a fire or a bullet…or worse.' Her bruised cheek ached with each word, her lip bled with the effort to speak.

Albero would be determined to get rid of any witnesses to Tiny's murder, especially when he'd been the one to hold the boy down while his partner, Serena Snow, administered the deadly overdose that killed his runner. Her husband had held Luke and forced him to watch, promising he'd be next if he didn't do as he was told.

'My handbag…where is it?' she asked suddenly, her heart in her throat.

He pulled it out of the cabinet next to her bed and

held it up. 'In here. I thought you might need it for identification.'

Oh God. Had he looked inside? Had he found the notebook? It was all there, recorded in Luke's diary along with dates and times of every delivery he'd done for his father, and the people who'd received them. All coded neatly so the untrained eye wouldn't see the subliminal messages, except for the moment when Tiny Watts was murdered. Her head pounded with pain as she tried to concentrate. If he found it and had it decoded —

His eyes narrowed on her face but all he said was, 'While you and Luke are here, you have round-the-clock guard. Depending on the autopsy findings and the judge's decision at the preliminary hearing, Luke could be placed in remand at the detention centre. We're expecting the autopsy results in by the end of the week.'

Lily drew in a shuddering breath. 'Remand? How well will he be protected from…the other inmates?'

'That depends on the level of danger he's in. Lily, if there is some reason you feel you or Luke are in danger, tell me please.'

'And where will he be until the hearing?' Her voice cracked and her eyes stung with unshed tears.

'When you're feeling up to it, I'll take your statement and we can get this under way. Once I have your statements, I'll submit the evidence. A lawyer from the district attorney's office is on his way now so he can be present when I interview Luke. He'll try to arrange a preliminary hearing via video link as soon as possible. We won't know where Luke will be placed until then.' The quiet reassurance in his voice did nothing to settle the nausea that rolled in her stomach.

'I need to see Luke.' She pushed the thin covering of the blanket away and pushed up off the pillows.

'Stay there, I'll open the curtain.' Mark stood and walked around the bed to sweep the curtain aside.

Lily turned her aching body toward the bed next to hers. Luke lay sleeping, curled up in foetal position, his bruises dark purple against his pale skin. The steady beep of his heart through the monitor and his gentle snoring reassured Lily he was still alive. She settled against the pillows, a sigh shuddering through her. Keeping him alive would be her next challenge.

'I'll give you my statement, Detective.' Lily's voice was faint but determined.

Mark sat and pulled his mobile phone from his pocket. 'Do you mind if we record the interview with this?' He held it up and wiggled it between long, strong fingers. 'It's much easier than taking notes and more reliable in case I miss something.'

Lily eyed him cautiously, her gaze taking in the strong contours of his face. The straight eyebrows and forehead — now marred by a frown — assured her he was a solid thinker who would consider all the facts first before passing judgement. She'd learned to read facial expressions and body language over the years…she'd had to with Gino. Without them, she would have a lot more scars. She'd learned when to steer clear of confrontation. God knows, it could have been her or Luke lying downstairs on a cold slab in the morgue if she hadn't learned when to back down. Still, could she trust this man who had the power to take everything they had left away from them?

'Whatever it takes.' She was so tired of running from the truth.

'Tell me what happened today.'

Lily sighed heavily. 'Gino's punch knocked me down. I fell and hit my head on the coffee table. It must have knocked me out for a bit.' Absently, she touched the tender spot near the top of her skull and felt a raw knot the size of a small egg.

'Your skin was split. They've glued the cut. How long do you think you were out for?'

'Not long. When I came around, Gino and Luke were fighting.' She shivered as she relived the scene in her head. Gino with his hands around Luke's neck...Luke's strength no match for anger. 'Luke couldn't breathe. I could see him turning blue from the force of Gino's hands around his neck. I tried to stop him and that's when I saw what Luke had in his hand. I don't know where he got it from.' She clutched the cold cotton of the hospital blanket like a lifeline thrown from a boat. The tears she'd held back trickled down her cheeks.

'Got what from?'

'The gun. Luke had a gun in his hand. It must be Gino's. I tried to stop them fighting, got between them. Gino made a grab for the gun, and it went off.' Her breath hitched and she closed her eyes. 'He fell.'

'So did Luke shoot Gino?' Mark's voice was soft, encouraging.

'No…I don't know…I…' She swiped at the tears on her cheeks. 'All three of us had our hands on the gun, Detective. When Gino grabbed Luke's hand, it went off.'

'Do you think Luke would shoot his father deliberately?'

Lily looked to where her hands gripped the sheet, knuckles white, shaking. If she said yes, she would incriminate him. She hesitated and looked at Mark, seeing nothing but a detective looking for answers, his face open and honest. Still the words hesitated on her tongue.

He met her gaze with empathy in his own. 'That wasn't a leading question, Lily. I'm trying to establish his state of mind. The two of you suffered trauma prior to the shooting. It makes a difference.'

Lily hesitated a moment longer. Her instinct said to trust him and that's all she had left. 'No. I think he was trying to scare Gino into backing off. You have no idea the torment he put us through.'

'Tell me,' Mark said.

As Lily opened her mouth to speak, Luke's voice whispered across the space between their beds. 'Mum.'

Lily sat up and swung her legs over the side of the bed. Dizziness hit her like a brick wall, and she sank back.

'Easy,' Mark warned, a hand at her waist for support as he pulled her drip stand closer.

She flinched away, the recoil automatic. Without a word she stood, slower this time. Using the drip stand for support, she walked the short distance to her son's side.

'I'm here, Luke.'

'You okay, Mum?'

'Yes, I'm okay. We're okay.'

'I'm sorry.'

Lily looked at her son, lying against the stark white pillows. Dark bruises and dried blood marred his otherwise flawlessly pale skin. His sharp cheekbones hollow in the harsh hospital lighting. He was a shadow of the happy little boy she'd once bounced on her knee and cuddled close at bedtime.

'It was an accident, Luke.' She pressed a kiss against his temple.

'But I *wanted* to kill him. Is it so bad to want to kill him after what he did to us?'

Lily ran a hand through his hair and stroked his forehead. 'He can't hurt us anymore, baby.'

'What will happen to us now?'

Lily looked at the detective, who stood silently at her side. His eyes met hers, empty of judgement and full of reassurance. 'We tell the truth and rebuild our lives… one brick at a time.' *And pray to God we stay alive long enough to live it.*

Silenced (Unfinished Business Book 3) can be purchased from your favourite bookseller. If they don't have it, ask them or your local library to order it in for you.

Dear Reader

This book has been written and edited using Australian / UK English grammar and punctuation conventions because the story is set in Australia. For more information on the differences between UK and US language and punctuation, please consider reading this article: https://tinyurl.com/56tkbh6a

If you enjoyed this book, please consider leaving a review on BookBub, Goodreads or the platform you purchased it from. If you would prefer to email me, please visit the contact page on my website at https://juanitakees.com/contact/. I do love to hear from readers and welcome your feedback.

Kind regards

Juanita Kees

Other Books by Juanita Kees

Wongan Creek Series

Whispers

Secrets

Shadows

Unfinished Business

Exposed

Tagged

Silenced

Bindarra Creek

Home to Bindarra Creek

Promise Me Forever

The Calhouns of Montana

Montana Baby

Montana Daughter

Montana Son

Contemporary Romance

Finish Line

Paranormal Fantasy

The Gods of Oakleigh

FINISHLINE - By Juanita Kees